I0822482

ANY LICH WAY

THE GOOD NECROMANCER

BOOK 6

MICHAEL LA RONN

Copyright © 2024 Michael La Ronn. All rights reserved.

Published by Author Level Up LLC.

Version 1.0

Cover design by MiBLArt.

Editing by BZ Hercules and Audrey Weinbrecht.

The characters and events in this book are fictitious. Any similarity to real persons, living or dead, is coincidental and not intended by the author.

No part of this book may be reproduced or used in any manner without written permission of the author except for the use of quotations in a book review.

Very special thanks to the following patrons who support the author on Patreon: Stephen Frans, Jon Howard, Michael Guishard, Beth Jackson, Lynda Washington, and Etta Welk.

For avoidance of doubt, Author reserves the rights, and no one has the rights to reproduce and/or otherwise use this work in any manner for purposes of training artificial intelligence technologies to generate text, including without limitation, technologies that are capable of generating works in the same style or genre as the work without the Author's specific and express permission to do so. Nor does any person or company have the right to sublicense others to reproduce and/or otherwise use this work in any manner for purposes of training artificial intelligence technologies to generate text without Author's specific and express permission.

CHAPTER ONE

THERE'S nothing like a late winter afternoon, a few days after the last snow of the year has fallen and spring has begun its slow, sometimes schizophrenic march toward green grass, clear skies, and radiant flowers.

It was the perfect day for a nap. I had just lit a fire in the living room and lain on my couch next to the windows. Slats of wintry sunlight sliced down through the blinds and across the floor. The fire crackled, flames pirouetting around the andirons. I imagined the boreal chill outside burning away as I cradled my head against my palms and rested my eyes.

Hazel, my German Shepherd Labrador mix, lay on her side at the base of the couch next to the radiator. Her brindled fur rustled gently from the radiator's toasty airflow. She didn't take long to frolic off to dreamland, because she blanketed the room with a steady cadence of snoring and an irregular whimper here and there. She must have been chasing a rabbit or something.

The flames from the fireplace cocooned me in a quilt of tingling warmth. I counted cars zipping by outside, tires scraping over the snow. Around the fifth car, I found myself somewhere between this world and the dreaming realm, consumed with that in-between sleepiness that can launch you into a lucid dream. You're not quite here, not quite there, and everything's quite all right.

Pure tranquility. Pure bliss. The only place I wanted to be at that very moment—here, in my 100-year-old home in the middle of the hood, my tiny slice of heaven.

Until my cell phone rang.

I like to call myself an experienced napper, but today, I made the rookie mistake of keeping my phone in my oxford pocket. Normally, I leave it on the kitchen table when I take naps, but I had been so sleepy that I slipped up on my protocol.

The phone vibrated violently and sent a shockwave across my chest, followed by an annoying metallic trill. I jumped up and the phone nearly fell out of my pocket.

Hazel jolted awake and stared at me sleepily, irritated from being pulled from dreamland so soon.

"Sorry, sweet pea," I said groggily.

My heart raced as a name flashed in bright white letters on the screen. Then, I relaxed a little.

It was my daughter, Marlese. Judging from California time, she was probably finishing a late breakfast. I imagined her sitting at her kitchen table, drenched in milky white California sunlight, balancing my grandson in her lap, her phone between her immaculate blue and black micro braids, as she called me.

"Hey, Mar," I said.

"You sleep?" Marlese asked. Her voice had its usual sardonic tone.

"Not anymore."

"You know, you don't have to answer the phone when you're taking a nap, Daddy," she said. "I was going to send you and Bo a text."

I ran my hand down my face as I yawned and re-accustomed myself to reality. A diagonal sunbeam warmed the back of my neck, and my phone's ringtone still trilled in my ears.

"Chalk it up to parental superstition," I said. "Never know when it could be an emergency."

"Since you're up, I wanted to give you details about the wedding. Can you write a few things down?"

Marlese was engaged to the father of her child, Darvin. She visited me last fall, and I met him and my grandson, Malcolm. Darvin was an Indian-haired, socially awkward guy with a goofy smile, but he treated my baby girl right, so he was okay with me. He asked me for her hand in marriage before he and Marlese flew back to LA. He spent the holiday season saving for a ring, working extra hours for a delivery company, and he finally proposed to Mar a few weeks ago. Mar called me every week to get feedback on the wedding. It was going to be a small ceremony in Santa Monica in the summer. And guess who was paying for it?

I grabbed a notebook and pen off a nearby lampstand. "I'm all ears, sweetheart."

Marlese took off, talking a mile a minute. "Remember that wedding expo I told you about? Darvin and I went last night. It inspired me with some ideas for decorations and centerpieces. I will send you some pictures. You *have* to share them with Mom and Nana, okay?"

I let out a little laugh. My wife Amira had to be in the spirit world, smiling. We were one lucky family. My daughter was getting wedding advice from beyond the grave.

Marlese stopped. "You there?"

"Here. Your mom and grandmother will be glad to give you advice. They liked the colors. Purple and gold. They suit you."

"Anyway, I've still got a lot of work to do, but I think I solved the tuxedo problem."

"Problem?"

"One word," Marlese said, sighing. I could practically

hear her lips wrinkling into exasperation on the other side of the phone. "Bo."

"Ah. That."

"If you go to the local tuxedo shop, he'll get some funny stares, and honestly, I don't think there's a single tux in *any* shop that would fit him. And if he has to take his clothes off..."

Bo was my undead servant, and he was every bit as undead as you could imagine. He's a spirit in a cadaver's body, and let's just say that when he takes his clothes off, it's not pretty. He looks like a science experiment, with stitches where the coroner cut into his corpse during the autopsy. I'll spare you the rest of the morbid details.

"I found a franchise out here in California that specializes in regular *and* big and tall sizes," Marlese went on. "They come to your house to get measurements so you don't have to go to the store. They even deliver the tux rentals to your house. Everything is done discreetly."

I grinned. Leave it to Marlese to think of details I hadn't considered. "Sounds like a plan. When do you want us to fly out?"

"That's the best part," Marlese said. "They have a franchise in St. Louis. I gave them your info, and they have an opening today. Is the house decent?"

I checked my watch. It was half past one. I didn't exactly feel like company today, but hopefully, it wouldn't take too long.

"Bo cleaned yesterday. We'll be ready."

I took the phone number of the tux guy, and I told Marlese to kiss my grandson for me.

I put my phone and notebook on the lampstand and settled back into the groove I had made on the couch. It was nice and warm, and before long, I was sinking into darkness.

At the beginning of my dream, I was lying on my couch. The walls shook. Somewhere nearby, something metallic clinked and dribbled across the floor with a high-pitched whine. Then—

Thump. Thump.

I inhaled nice and slow, and ignored it.

Thump.

Somewhere, a deep voice shouted.

"Get over here, you little punk!"

It was Bo. The walls vibrated, and he let out an angry war cry.

My eyes snapped open. I wasn't dreaming.

"Naw, dog. Come out and fight like a man!"

Irritation washed over me in a great wave of fire. "Bo, what the hell is going on over there?"

No answer. Just another thump.

"Argh!" Bo cried.

Seconds later, the pocket door to the living room rumbled aside, and Bo peeked his bald head in. Today, he wore a track-suit whose color scheme could best be described as "ketchup and mustard." The bright colors hitting my eyes helped me confirm I was awake. The big man's mouth was contorted into a scowl. He pointed one of my boots at me.

"I've had it, boss man," he said. "Unless you want me to burn this house down, you better call an exterminator."

I groaned. "*Another* cockroach?"

"Tryin' to mooch off the soup on the stove, no less," Bo said.

"Why do you have to use one of my boots?" I asked, bristling at the thought of cleaning a flattened cockroach off the sole.

A furious fluttering erupted from the kitchen. I would have taken it for a bird if I didn't know any better.

Bo sprinted into the kitchen. "Back for another round?" he said loudly. "Let's go. Uh huh—yeah, baby, you're going down!"

Hazel tilted her head at me and let out a quiet whine.

"At least *you* made it to dreamland," I said, rising.

Our German cockroach debacle started a few days ago. While doing laundry one night, I caught a pair coming up through a sewer grate in the basement. And those were just the ones I *saw*. Bo and I have been living in misery ever since.

Don't get the wrong idea about me. Cockroaches aren't unheard of around here, but I keep a clean house. Until now, this place had never seen a rat or a roach. These guys' very existence was an affront to my upbringing. I sent my gang of undead spiders after them, but these cockroaches were twice their size.

Bo and I fought the good fight, but it was time to accept that we were losing.

The walls shook.

"Ha ha haaaa!"

Bo did a victory dance in the kitchen like a football player in the end zone after a touchdown. The nylon on his tracksuit rubbed together like leaves. He waved my boot and talked to a brown mass oozing on the sole.

"This is my house. My house!"

"And that's *my* boot," I said.

"Small price to pay to protect the soup," Bo said, pointing to a homemade chicken noodle soup he had been brewing on the stove in a stainless steel stock pot. The kitchen was steeped in the nose-watering aroma of chicken, celery, carrots, and—you won't believe this—Tabasco sauce. Shocked the hell out of me too, but Bo's recipe was delicious. The perfect meal for a cold wintry day.

Bo opened the back door to the porch and chucked my shoe out. "I'll get it cleaned up in a bit, boss man. Gotta finish the soup."

I couldn't believe Bo had dragged me off the couch for this. I told him about the tuxedo man.

"Mar's always thinkin' ahead," Bo said, tapping his forehead. He gave the soup a vigorous stir. "That tux man is going to have an impossible job, and for that, I salute him."

"I'm going back to sleep until he gets here," I said. "Don't wake me again unless it's the apocalypse."

"Depends on your definition of apocalypse," Bo said, giving me an ugly grin.

"I'm talking archangels, clarions, and walls of fire," I said, waving him away as I padded back down the hallway.

"A'ight. Whatever you say."

Bo switched on the radio on the counter and went back to chopping onions, dancing in place to the beats of Dr. Dre.

I eased into the couch again and closed my eyes. Nothing was going to stop me this time. I breathed in deep and wiggled back into the groove.

A minute later, screeching tires howled across the street. Then—

Zzzzzzzt!

Lightning bolts shot through my skull. Every square inch of my scalp whistled electric as a kaleidoscope of black-and-white images spun around my mind's eye like a whirling dervish, wild at the edges, then sharpening into view.

My front porch spider was on high alert. It spotted a visitor and beamed me its sight from its perch in the cavity just above the screen door.

An oversized white cargo van had jumped the curb in front of my house. Thank goodness there was snow on the ground because it would have destroyed my grass otherwise. The van beeped. The bumper spat out snow and the van dropped a few inches with a loud, clattering thunk. Then, the driver straightened the van out.

A few long seconds later, a gangly man with thickly moussed hair climbed out—rather, swirled—out of the car. He wore a pinstriped vest and black dress pants that were perfectly tailored. He wobbled for a moment, then balanced himself, adjusting a long swath of measuring tape wrapped around his neck like a python.

The man examined his parking job, shrugged, and flung the cargo van open, unleashing a metallic peal that echoed up and down the street.

My spider's heartbeat synced with mine. The Cluster didn't like visitors unless they were on my very small VIP list.

I opened my eyes and shot up.

"Bo!" I shouted. "Tux man's here."

"Bet," Bo said, clanking around in the kitchen.

Hazel lay on the floor, her ears down. She whimpered again.

"So much for naptime, sweet pea," I said. "I need to see a man about a tux."

I guess it really was true that you could sleep when you were dead.

CHAPTER TWO

"MARLESE SHO' knows how to pick 'em," Bo said as we took turns at the peephole. "Mmm mmm mmm. Who let *this* dude out of the freak show?"

Bo wasn't always articulate with his words, but he wasn't lying. It was cold enough outside for a thick winter coat, yet the man dressed like it was spring. Heaven knows how someone could have missed the weather report on a day like this.

I noticed more details about him now that I was seeing him with my own eyes. His vest was a pop of red and gold, and you could have seen him half a mile away. His silver moussed hair reminded me of a lion's mane. Every step he made around the van was a swirl. The man was light on his feet.

The gangly man rooted around in the cargo van for a quick minute, pushing hanging tuxedos aside before emerging with a leather garment bag in one hand and an enormous black shell case that was as long as he was tall. He slammed the cargo van door, revealing the name of the company in plain black letters against the white paint: Whispering Pines

Tuxedo Company. He lumbered unsteadily toward the steps with the garment bag and shell case in hand.

"What do you think is in that case?" Bo asked.

"Your shame," I said, frowning. "Give the man some grace."

Bo scratched his bald head. "A'ight. But you're thinking the same thing I am."

"Maybe," I said, "but the world has enough bad juju out there, so I'm holding my tongue."

"Juju or not, your boy is strange as hell, and that's just the truth, boss man," Bo said, shaking his head.

As the man wobbled up the stairs, Bo opened the door in anticipation.

"Need help, dog?"

The man struggled up the stairs, barely keeping his balance, but somehow, he made it. Sweat beaded his brow as he set the giant case down on the porch concrete and panted. "Thank you, sir, but the hard work is done now."

He had the air of a circus ringmaster. The only thing missing was a baton, elephants, and a background of marquee lights. He wore a thick mustache that was almost completely gray except for a few black strands. His red and gold vest was even brighter up close. A wide smile spread across his paper-white face as he finally caught his breath.

"My deepest apologies for running over your curb," he said between breaths. "My van sometimes has an energy all its own."

"You didn't hit the fire hydrant, so we good," Bo said, grinning his usual ugly grin.

"Where are my manners?" the man asked, taking Bo's hand and shaking it effusively. "Mr. Broussard, it is my pleasure. I want to thank you for your business. I can't tell you how much it means to me that your daughter has chosen my company to outfit you for her special day."

The man spoke quietly but full of conviction, full of zest.

He reminded me of an academic—perfect diction, every syllable pronounced.

"Sup," Bo said. "But I ain't Mr. Broussard."

"That would be me," I said, extending my hand.

Embarrassment splashed across the gangly man's face. "So sorry. So sorry. I must have mixed up my notes, Mr. Holloway."

He quickly took my hand and pumped it. His handshake was firm and warm. "I had the pleasure of speaking with your daughter Marlese by telephone. What a delightful young woman with excellent taste."

The man stepped back and gave a slight bow. "I am Orman Misterka with The Whispering Pines Tuxedo Company, at your service for the next thirty minutes. May I come in, Mr. Broussard?"

I gestured him in, and Bo held the door as he gangled into the house with the suitcase, his arms swinging the case and garment bag and his long legs moving slightly out of sync. As he passed the threshold, Bo gave me a lingering look with wrinkled lips that telegraphed "I told you this dude was crazy." I mouthed silently for him to be quiet.

I directed Misterka to the living room, where Hazel greeted him and sniffed the shell case. I told her to stand down and she took her spot on the floor by the radiator.

"You've created a proper place indeed for a fitting," Misterka said, glancing at the fireplace. The living room *was* cozy, though the fire needed more wood. The air was laced with the red-hot aroma of soup from the kitchen. I was suddenly hungry, and I wished this fitting would be done already.

Misterka lugged the shell onto my rug in the center of the living room, unlatched it, unfolded a huge trifold vanity mirror, and snapped angled metal legs into place. I saw myself in triplicate standing in the pocket door threshold.

"So that's what that is," Bo said.

Misterka gave Bo a wry grin. "Yes—this usually keeps my customers guessing. It's to ensure you two will look your absolute best on Marlese's special day."

I went first. He had me change into a white tuxedo shirt and a sample jacket. He measured me as I stood in front of the trifold mirror with my arms outstretched. He worked with such a lightning rapidity that it was impossible to know where the man's hands were. If this were a cartoon, he would have surrounded me in a furious cloud with his hands everywhere at the same time. The measuring tape clicked and rasped as he worked it around my neck, my torso, and down my waist. The man rattled off numbers between moments of silence and small talk, mostly about the weather. I felt the occasional poke of a pin and the scratch of chalk against fabric on my skin as he marked off measurements.

"You're going to look marvelous, Mr. Broussard," Misterka said as I returned the sample tuxedo shirt and jacket to him. "Simply marvelous."

And then there was Bo. Let's just say that he was a project. Misterka had to measure his waist several times. ("You're a man of much difficulty, Mr. Holloway.") I didn't know if they made neckties big enough for guys like Bo. ("Your neckwear will require extra fabric, but don't despair!")

And the shoes. Don't get me started on the shoes. You know those surveys where they ask you a question and they give you the choice to select Other - please specify? Bo's shoe size was definitely "Other." And if I had to specify, I would say his feet were the size of barges. ("My, my, my. There are feet, and then there are *your* feet, Mr. Holloway. No offense meant, of course.")

Bo had a shirt disaster too. He insisted on wearing an undershirt under the sample tuxedo shirt because—you know, reasons—but Misterka wouldn't have it.

"It will put off my numbers too much," he said, furrowing

his brow. "It won't do. It's quite all right. Marlese told me that you had some…medical conditions."

The gangly man held up his hands upon realizing his poor choice of words, the measuring tape dangling like a sleeping cobra. "Now now, she didn't tell me what they were. It's none of my business. However, if I am to give you the best tuxedo of your life, you must trust me."

Misterka made prayer hands. "I hope my actions up to this point have conveyed my trustworthiness."

Bo glanced at me. I nodded to him. A few minutes later, he stood in front of the trifold mirror in his drawers and the biggest poplin tuxedo shirt I'd ever seen. It could have been a bedsheet. His stitches and autopsy cuts were visible through the shirt. Misterka saw them, but he said nothing as he wrapped the measuring tape around Bo's waist.

"Yes, we're making progress, Mr. Holloway. I think we can find a workable solution. No problem is too big and no man is too tall for The Whispering Pines Tuxedo Company."

At last, Misterka held up a note card he had used to take measurements and flicked it with two fingers. "Congratulations, gentlemen. You're one step closer to looking the best you've ever looked in your lives."

With astonishing quickness, he latched the black shell case and hung the sample tuxedo shirts and jackets in the garment bag. After he finished, he stood with the case and garment bag in hand, staring at me. His mustache was twitching. The length of the stare made me uncomfortable, like he was staring through me. His air had changed, like he was irritated at me.

"Something wrong, Mr. Misterka?" I asked.

"It appears you have an unwelcome guest," he said wanly, pointing at the cockroach crawling up the wall behind the couch. Its wings clicked together and it looked ready to take flight.

"Aw, hell naw," Bo said.

The next thing I knew, Bo dove through the air with a napkin and snatched the bugger off the wall. He crumpled the napkin, killing the roach with a satisfying crisp.

“Heh,” Bo said when he realized Misterka was staring at him oddly. “Minor pest control problem.”

Misterka’s stare remained—this time not at Bo, but on the wall at the brown spot where some of the roach remained. I sure as heck didn’t want to know what he was thinking about me. My stomach churned with embarrassment.

Finally, the gangly man shrugged. “I suppose death is the appropriate penalty for trespassing.”

“You got that right,” I said.

Bo and I escorted the gangly man to the door.

"I thank you kindly,” he said with a quarter bow.

"What do I owe you?" I asked, pulling out my wallet.

"Nothing at all, Mr. Broussard. You'll pay after you've tried on your tuxedo. If you don't like how you look, it's free."

I've rented tuxes before. I always had to make a down payment or pay a fee upfront. But hey, I wasn't going to argue with the guy. These days, a man ought to save every buck he can.

Misterka bade us farewell for the second time and grunted as he hauled the black shell case and garment bag down the steps on my front porch.

“You sure you don’t want help?” Bo asked.

“I must earn my bread, Mr. Holloway,” Misterka said.

Bo saluted and disappeared into the house to tend to the soup.

I was just about to shut the door when a frightened cry ripped across the porch.

It happened in slow motion: Misterka tumbling in midair like a terrible acrobat. The garment bag fluttering in the wind and landing in the snow. The black shell case hurtling toward the ground. The glass inside shattering and bouncing around the inside of the shell like rocks. Misterka landing on his shoulder first, his body making a sickening crunch. His head slamming against the concrete. Then, the stunned man rolling head over heels down each step like a slinky.

Then, time stopped for a moment and it was just me on the threshold watching, the gunmetal sky overhead that seemed to close in like a pillow ready for the smother, and Misterka on the ground like a rag doll, his lanky legs twisted beneath him.

"Sheeeeet!" I cried, tearing the screen door open.

"Bo. Bo!"

Bo peeked his head out of the kitchen. "What?"

"Bo!" I cried nervously as I dashed across the porch. I damn near slipped down the steps and fell onto Misterka.

Then Bo saw the carnage.

"Gaaaahdamn—" Bo shouted, rocketing out of the house.

I grabbed Misterka by the shoulder. His eyes were closed.

"Orman," I said softly but firmly. "Mr. Misterka."

He was out like a light.

I checked his pulse. Faint, but he was alive. I straightened out his legs, but I didn't move him from his twisted angle on the stairs for fear of a spine injury.

"Call an ambulance and get a blanket," I told Bo. He obliged.

An icy gust ripped through me as I sat with the gangly man and said his name. He would not wake. His face was covered with a rash of cuts, blisters, and bumps from the rough concrete. Bo and I covered him with a blanket and said nothing as seconds felt like hours.

My stomach twisted into knots and every muscle in my body went taut as piano wire.

Things weren't looking so good for Misterka.

CHAPTER THREE

THE POLICE, fire department, and paramedics came right away. Before long, the street was aswirl with sirens and flashing lights. And, of course, everyone on the block gawked from their porches as Misterka lay unconscious on the cement.

I had stayed with the man, holding one of his hands, trying to get him to wake up. His thickly moussed silver hair was a mop atop his head now. One of the buttons had popped off his red and gold vest, and the vest flapped in the breeze.

When the paramedics took over, I was trembling. My hands wouldn't stop shaking and I couldn't stop thinking that this man was going to die. Bo and I watched stupefied as the paramedics lifted Misterka onto a stretcher and transported him away with sirens blaring.

The fact that there were sirens at all made me feel a little better. Last year, one of my elderly neighbors fell and hit his head in the middle of the night. The fall sent him into cardiac arrest. When the ambulance, firefighters, and police left, it was like a silent funeral procession. Standing then on the porch in the cool summer night, Bo and I had known that Mr. Jacobson had departed for the spirit world.

Maybe Misterka had a chance.

"Anything else you can tell me?" a black police officer asked, eager to write the details down as we stood on the porch.

Bo and I told him everything that had happened—that the gangly man was a little unsteady coming up the stairs, and that we offered to help him on his way back to the van, but he refused. I could tell the officer felt sorry for me.

"Is there any way I can visit him in the hospital?" I asked.

The officer tucked his notepad into his uniform chest pocket. "I'd give the doctors some time. His injuries looked pretty bad. You might try going up to the hospital later tonight before visiting hours are over to ask about him, but you might not get far. Judging from the situation, he'll probably be in intensive care."

The officer said a few kind words to me and Bo. Then he got into his car and drove away, leaving me staring after him.

Bo went inside. Only then did I realize that I had been outside all this time without a coat. The chill hit me like a bomb.

I was about to go inside to warm up when an elderly voice called to me.

"Bad day, baby?"

I turned to the house on my right, a gray brick three-story home with pointed dormers on the third floor.

My neighbor, Granny, sat in her lawn chair on her porch. Granny was my mother's best friend, and she was like a second mother to me. She wore a stocking cap over big silver curls, and what looked like one of her grandson's safety orange puffer jackets over one of her trademark floral smocks. She hugged herself, shivering.

"Hey, Granny."

"If you need a witness, I saw it all," she said. "Couldn't help but notice all the activity over at your place." Her usual calm face snapped into her hard gossip mode. "That man tripped over his own feet and fell down your stairs like a box of rocks. Don't let nobody tell you otherwise."

I dug my hands into my pockets to warm them up. "Who do I have to convince?"

"That man don't look like no spring chicken, but he also don't look like he qualifies for Medicare and Social Security either, you know what I'm saying?"

I stared at her. I had no idea what she was saying.

"You need yourself a good lawyer, Lester Broussard," Granny said, frowning at me. "Folks around here are liable to get ideas once medical bills come due."

I sighed as if Granny had punched me in the gut. I knew what she was talking about now.

You see, the city of St. Louis is what you might call a judicial hellhole. Everybody sues everybody for every little thing, and the courts let people get away with it. Turn on the TV here, and every other commercial is an advertisement for a law firm promising to get you every penny you deserve.

Lawyers... Good Lord.

"You remember George Decker? Cab driver that stayed 'round the way on Kensington?" Granny continued. "He had a family barbecue a couple years back. One of his nephews invited a friend, who invited a girlfriend. At least that's how I think it was. This girl fell down the stairs and broke—her—neck. Needed care for life. Sued him for two million! *You know* George Decker ain't got that kinda money. No insurance, neither. Had to file for bankruptcy. Last I heard, the girl done put a lien on the poor man's house."

"Sheeeeet," I said. "Look at my steps, Granny. There's nothing wrong with them. I had them repaved last year. Not a single crack."

"Wasn't nothing wrong with George Decker's staircase either," Granny said with a long face.

I shook my head. "Thanks for the advice, but I need to lie down."

"You *need* a good lawyer," Granny insisted. "Don't be stubborn about this. Doesn't your...*friend* know anybody?"

A pregnant pause hung between us. I was going to be sick, and her offhand comment especially didn't help.

The truth was that Granny and I had grown apart since I had gotten back into necromancy. Granny is an old-fashioned kind of woman. Strong-willed. God-fearing. All the supernatural stuff wouldn't sit well with her, and I guess, subconsciously, I'd gone out of my way to keep her out of it.

Plus, Granny didn't like Bo. It started when she made us a plate of hot chicken and black-eyed peas. Granny sat and visited with us for a while. Bo didn't touch his plate. The dead man couldn't eat, after all, but we couldn't exactly tell her that. For a woman like Granny, to not eat her food is an assault against every ounce of her being. Cooking is how she shows her affection.

She had been chilly to Bo ever since. I sure as heck didn't feel like re-litigating her grievances with him right now.

"You keep me posted," she said.

"Nothing's going to happen, Granny."

I waved her away, stumbled into the house, and found my way to the couch. I closed my eyes and massaged my temples.

I couldn't stop thinking about what Granny said. *Did* I need a lawyer? Was Misterka going to sue me? If he did, what the hell was I going to say?

My stomach rumbled. I was hungry, yet stress made me reluctant to eat. Between thinking about my pending legal issues and images of Misterka's body crunching down my steps, I couldn't sleep either.

I just hoped he would be okay. He seemed like a nice guy. A little eccentric, but really into his job. Before he left, I had no doubt that he would have dressed me and Bo to the nines.

And his family. Didn't he have a family? A wife? Children? They would be devastated. I felt the pain that they were sure to feel when the police notified them that he was in the hospital, likely hooked up to dozens of tubes in the intensive care unit.

I resolved to visit him later. This was going to gnaw away at me until I knew for sure how he was. Part of me didn't want to see him, though.

Granny's voice echoed through my head. She had a way of getting in there.

"You need yourself a good lawyer, Lester Broussard…"

Sighing, I decided that there was no downside to assuming Granny was right. I called the only person I knew who might be able to help.

"Lester, what a rare occasion," Detective Damian Harris said over the phone.

Harris was a baby-faced detective in the St. Louis Police Department Paranormal Crimes Division, and he had saved my life on more than one occasion. We were friends.

"I need a favor."

I told him everything and he listened without saying a word.

"Wow," he said finally, trying to suppress a chuckle. "If it weren't for bad luck, you wouldn't have any."

"You sound like my neighbor," I said.

"I know a good defense lawyer. He handles these types of things. He's not cheap, but he's not the most expensive guy in town either. He owes me a favor. Maybe I can get you some legal hours pro bono or something."

"I can't thank you enough," I said.

"Don't mention it."

He paused. "Say, Lester, while I've got you on the phone...."

Here we went again. I was asking him a favor, but I didn't

seriously think he would ask to cash it in so soon. But I had to hear him out.

"Last year, I made you an offer about being a paid paranormal consultant with the PD."

Imagine me, helping cops solve murders. No sir, no way. Sure, the money would have been nice, but that kind of thing didn't light me up. Plus, I didn't want folks in the neighborhood to see me working with the police. That didn't go well around here.

"I told you, I would love to help you, but—"

"I didn't expect you to change your mind," Harris said. "But I am dealing with a rather sticky situation right now. I wouldn't mind some good old-fashioned friend-to-friend advice. Plus, this has no strings to anything in your neighborhood. It's in the county."

The offer didn't sound too bad.

"Murder?" I asked.

"There are words that describe things," Harris said wistfully. "I don't know if murder describes this one."

"What do you need?"

"To review some pictures. I am stumped with a capital S. I need an experienced necromancer's eye."

Harris was a necromancer too. He was still learning the dark art, but he should have given himself more credit.

I was bound to oblige. In the paranormal world, favors carry weight. If you do something for someone, you are obligated to return the favor with a commensurate act. I could look at some pictures and offer advice, no problem. Struck me as a win-win.

Harris gave me an address and time, and I told him I'd be there.

CHAPTER FOUR

Bo and I waited for Harris in a pancake house parking lot on the north side of town by the airport. The interstate had taken us far from the heart of the city where I lived and into the quasi-suburbs. Yet, my 1993 Lincoln Town Car still fit in with the mixture of old and modern cars in the lot.

I tried to take my mind off Misterka. Bo helped me accomplish that pretty quick by blaring his rap music.

I lost a bet against Bo, one that I regretted. During our last adventure, I showed a moment of weakness and let him listen to rap music in the car. Now, I let him play it every now and then. This was one of those times. Instead of thinking about Misterka's tumbling body and unconscious face, I couldn't stop thinking about how much I disliked Bo's music.

A specimen from one of his choices today? A woman rapping about her juice. As to what the juice is, I'll leave that to your imagination—but it ain't the kind you pour in a glass, if you know what I mean.

Despite the chest-rattling, braggadocious poetry that Bo had chosen, he succeeded in taking my mind off Misterka. Maybe that was why he suggested listening to rap today. He tapped the steering wheel, nodding in his sunglasses. His red track suit was so loud, you could spot him from the interstate a mile away.

He was also thoughtful enough to put some of his delicious Tabasco chicken noodle soup in an insulated canister for me to eat while we waited for Harris. When I say it was delicious, I mean it was spoon-slurping delicious. The Tabasco sauce tingled on my tongue—in a good way. It's a shame the pages of this book aren't scratch, sniff, and eat.

I was getting dizzy, and I forced myself to eat. I scooped the soup from the canister and tilted it high until the last salty, Tabasco-y drop of broth splashed on my tongue.

We sat, watching people stream in and out of the little triangle-shaped pancake house. It was a 24/7 joint. To say it was busy was an understatement. The smell of fried dough and bacon was heavy in the air, and I could smell it even with the car windows rolled up.

"I can't believe I said it," Bo said, tapping the steering wheel gently and shaking his head.

"Said what?"

"I said Misterka was from the freak show."

Ah, the bad juju. Bo had been pretty judgy about Misterka when he walked into the house. So was I.

"Now the man's lying in a hospital bed, man. I should've been nicer to him."

"We'll get a chance to make amends when we visit him later today," I said, propping my fist on my cheek as I stared blankly out the window.

"Yeah. We gotta look out for the guy. He got hurt on our property. That makes us responsible in some way, doesn't it?"

I closed my eyes. "Morally, sure, but hopefully not legally."

A black government sedan made a sharp turn into the parking lot. Harris spotted us and parked with his driver's side facing me on the passenger side.

I cranked my window just as the automatic window on Harris's window whirred down.

Harris leaned out. His black hair was neatly styled into a subtle upward swirl. He had just gotten out of the shower and smelled like laundry-scented bar soap and pomade. Today, he was wearing a tailored black suit, crisp white shirt, and shiny black tie. Typical detective get-up. He had a boyish gleam in his eyes and a manila envelope in one hand.

"You sure picked a happening place," I said. "I didn't know people were this crazy about pancakes."

"It's the rush hour," Harris said. "This place runs circles around all the chains. It's a regular hangout for some of the cops. In other words, about the safest meeting place I can think of, other than the station."

Harris slipped me a piece of paper scissored between two fingers. It had a name and phone number on it. An Arthur Arquette, Esq. I thanked him and slipped the paper into my pocket.

Harris gave a chin-up nod to Bo, and Bo returned the gesture.

"Sup, Harris. You're looking awfully young today."

"And you're looking awfully dead."

Bo thought about the comment for a second, then tapped his bald head and pointed at Harris jokingly.

Harris slipped me the envelope. "Fair warning that what's in there isn't pretty."

I gave Harris a lingering glance before grabbing my glasses out of my breast pocket and slipping them on.

I dragged a series of 8.5 x 11, glossy printed photographs out of the envelope.

The first was of a vomit-green door with brass numbers. A scarlet streak angled across the door in a diagonal, like an artist dragging a paintbrush across a canvas and running out of paint halfway through.

It was blood.

The picture was taken in what appeared to be low light, probably at night. The camera was a digital camera, but not a terribly high-quality one. Some of the pixels were a little blurry.

"I'm just getting you warmed up," Harris said.

Slowly, I pulled up the next photograph. It looked like an apartment bedroom. A twin bed next to a window with cheap dollar store curtains and a desk with a laptop computer on it. At the bottom of the frame were two bare white feet, placed as if the photographer almost missed them. There were golden speckles in the air, as if the air had been laced with glitter. Instinctively, I touched the photograph but quickly realized that the speckling was inherent in the image itself, not a quality of the printed paper.

"That fooled me too," Harris said. "Keep going."

The third photograph was of the body. Rather, what was left of it. It made me wish I hadn't eaten before Harris arrived. It was a Caucasian man, presumably in his thirties or forties by the look of him. He wore a basketball jersey, gym shorts, and a cloth bracelet around one wrist.

I wish I could have described his face to you, but he didn't have one. His head had exploded as if it were a giant pressure cooker with a clogged vent. He lay on the hardwood floor inside a terribly scrawled magic circle whose inner circle was broken.

Bo saw the image and turned away. "Aw, damn."

"Amateur necromancer," I said. "He didn't construct his circle correctly." I pointed a pinky at the outer circle, which was slightly elliptical. "He didn't measure it right. His outer circle messed up his inner one. He must have had poor depth perception."

"No doubt about it," Harris said.

"And a bedroom," I said, returning to the second image. "Unwise setting for a circle."

Harris raised an eyebrow.

"There are too many emotions in a bedroom," I said. "If you think about it, you spend a third of your day there.

Dreams and nightmares leave an emotional residue that we can't see. It's like a smorgasbord for demons. They'll know everything about you before you even open your mouth. Combine that with a raggedy circle, and you have your man here, Harris."

"Freaking amateurs," Harris said.

"Is he the type that dabbled in the dark art on the weekends?" Bo asked.

"Not exactly," Harris said. "This guy was a believer. Though he didn't have much skill, we found occult stuff all over his house. Spell books, scholarly texts on spirituality, the whole shebang."

"That's how it always starts," I said.

It took me back to my early days as a necromancer. Me and my friend CeCe studying magic books in her garage and learning how to communicate with the dead by experimenting with every technique we could find. It was dumb luck that I didn't end up like this guy with my head missing, with three people sitting in a pancake house parking lot trying to guess how I died.

"That's not all," Harris said. His voice took on a somber tone. I didn't like the shift.

"Look at the final photograph, Lester."

Reluctantly, I pulled out the final glossy picture. It was one of the man's hands. A golden wedding band was a dull hunk of metal around the ring finger. My eyes picked up on a silver chain that started at the man's wrist and flowed into his palm, where several viridian triangles of stained glass caught what little was left of the moonlight.

I followed the light rays outward until I made out the shape of an angled, springbox leg and a mosaicked, triangular wing. Then, surrounded by golden speckles—a blood-red eye that glowed as if it were alive.

It was a suncatcher. Of a grasshopper.

CHAPTER FIVE

"THE ANNOYING GRASSHOPPER STRIKES AGAIN," Bo said.

I sat, stunned.

The suncatcher of the grasshopper only meant one thing: Natkaal was involved.

Natkaal was a grasshopper demon, and we had a checkered history. When I first met him, he was what could best be described as a neutral, mischievous force. He helped me on numerous occasions. He saved my grandson from sure death during molting season, the time when archdemons swarm the spirit world.

I had been foolish enough to consider him a friend, and I realized that it was all a ruse. Or, at least, I think it was. I never really knew for sure. Everything Natkaal did, he did because he was under the influence of a curse that changed his nature from evil to quasi-good. When the curse was lifted, he returned to his usual demon ways. It left me shattered, betrayed, and feeling as if I had learned nothing about fooling around with the supernatural these past few years.

Seeing his presence in the photograph was like seeing a friend who had betrayed you the first time after the betrayal. It made me light-headed and weak.

"I don't know what the grasshopper is up to," Harris said, snapping me out of my thoughts. "But as usual, it's strange."

Harris's cell phone chirped. He glanced at the screen before silencing it.

"Do you think Natkaal killed that guy?" Bo asked.

"That's what I can't figure out," Harris said.

"Maybe he wanted to escape back into the world of the living," Bo said.

Demons don't belong in this world, and their presence here causes problems. Trust me, I would know. I stared at the photograph of the dead man lying on the floor in the magic circle, racking my brain about what the grasshopper could possibly be up to.

Harris ran a hand through his immaculate black hair. "I'm certain Natkaal is not among us. Apparently, he's the new sheriff in the spirit world. I talked to a few spirits, and he's got many of the biggest, baddest demons running scared. Those arrogant insect assholes are as meek as mice now. Can you believe shrimpy little *Natkaal* can make them do that? You couldn't get a demon to intervene in a séance if you wanted to these days, even if you called their names."

"Except for *this* séance," I said, pointing to the dead man.

Harris shrugged.

"Natkaal wants to become an archdemon," I said. "He made that clear. Anything he does, it's for that goal. Rounding up the demons under a new order is sure to get the attention of the council of archdemons during the next molting season. It might also restore his reputation among the archdemons. They're not fans of him. They consider him to be a traitor."

Harris hadn't considered that. "That's a good point, but why was this guy a casualty?"

I stared at the photograph of the dead man again. I focused on the suncatcher and glinting moonlight across its surface. Whatever it was, it had something to do with this mess.

Then I shuffled back to the first photograph of the door with the blood streak. I put both photos side-by-side on my thighs and looked back and forth between the dead man and the door. Then, I studied the golden speckles.

"Whatever our dead man did, he brought something into this world." I pointed at the blood streak on the door. "Maybe not Natkaal, but one of his minions." I shuddered at the thought of Natkaal having minions.

I organized the photographs in the same order that Harris had given them to me and tucked them neatly into the envelope before handing it back. "That's all I can tell you."

I frowned as I recalled the grasshopper demon's toothy smile full of triangular teeth. "Be careful. You know how unpredictable Natkaal can be," I said.

Harris saluted me and said he'd be in touch.

I was about to bid him goodbye when the sky darkened outside, like someone had drawn a giant curtain over the sun. The sky grew black—the pitch black you see in forests where the canopy is so thick that no moonlight can penetrate it.

Bo took off his sunglasses and squinted out the windshield. "What the—"

My heart sank as the air rippled, like someone had cupped a giant glass over the top of the parking lot. Bo's voice escaped into the air and died somewhere just past the pancake house. A wall of bubbling shadows veined with lightning sprang up, shrouding the premises.

I knew this magic. I'd seen it during my last adventure. It was called shadowcraft, and it was one of the most lethal forms of supernatural intentions.

Ahead, two black men were coming out of the pancake house. They were frozen in place—mouths in mid-talk and arms and legs locked in mid-stride like a freeze-frame.

I glanced at Harris. "Get ready!"

A whistling started high above us like a firework. It quickly turned into horrific screaming, like an angry teapot blowing its lid. The sound drenched the sky until it seeped into my bones and drew my eyes upward.

A boiling spear of golden light as tall as a telephone pole hurtled down from the sky. On the tip of the spear was a sharp face with serrated teeth moving among the plasma.

It laughed as it raced toward us.

CHAPTER SIX

THE LIGHT SPEAR broke right and zoomed toward Harris's sedan.

"Harris, get out!" I cried.

Bo dove out of my Lincoln Town Car, and I followed him, landing hard on my elbows.

Harris had his gun in hand. He dove out of the car just as the light spear pierced the ceiling of his government sedan. The car crumpled like a handful of leaves.

The light buzz-sawed the crumpled car in half, shearing the metal as the face gnashed its teeth. The car dissolved into golden speckles that lighted across the air before the spear blew a great gust across the parking lot, dispersing them.

Bo, Harris, and I regrouped in the middle of the parking lot, panting.

"Something tells me bullets won't work on this thing," Harris said, cocking his pistol, "but I'm going to try anyway."

I scanned the parking lot. I knew this magic. It was called shadowcraft. It stopped time and allowed the caster to act in secret and escape unpunished. I had encountered it while fighting a coven of elderly witches who used it to try to kill me. The magic was so powerful that it siphoned the very life force out of you. You literally threw away time and energy from your life to use it.

But this style of witchcraft required you to be near your intended mark. You couldn't just cast a shadowcraft spell and hope for the best from the safety of your armchair.

Yet, the parking lot was empty.

"Heads up, boss man!" Bo said, pushing me down.

The light spear zipped around the parking lot, then between Bo and me before circling back and zooming at us again.

Harris, with implacable resolve, crouched and fired two shots. The gunshots rang out hollow against the wall of shadows, and the wall quickly swallowed the noise.

The bullets ripped through the spear, diverting it high into the sky over the roof of the pancake house.

"I'll be damned," Harris said, grinning. "For once, my gun works!"

The spear latched one end to the sloped roof of the pancake house, reared up, and lashed down at Harris like a whip. It struck him in the chest and sent him flying. He crashed into the wall of shadows and landed face-first on the asphalt.

He groaned and tried to get up, but the spear had winded him.

Instinctively, I dashed toward Harris. The spear reared back and prepared a finishing lash. I slipped a razor blade out of my pocket.

I jumped in front of Harris's body. I was ready to cut a hole to the spirit world and send this thing back to wherever the hell it belonged.

The spear stopped mid-rear. Instead, it roared, shaking the ground and the cars nearby.

"Who are you?" I shouted.

The light spear roared again, baring its triangular teeth at me. It wanted me out of the way.

Bo joined me. "Answer the man's question!" he said.

The spear reared back again. This time, it hurled at us but stopped just before our faces. Its blinding light made me put my arm over my face to protect my eyes as it chomped its teeth at me. Its teeth clanged together like something striking the side of a dumpster with a metal pole.

"It doesn't want us," I said incredulously, loudly enough for Bo to hear over the racket.

It wanted Harris.

We had to take this spell out, quick.

The spear regrouped and skated across the sloped roof. It was thinking. Somehow, I had thwarted its plan.

I scanned the area again, looking for clues. I settled on one of the windows of the pancake house. A yellow shape moved inside.

I realized how stupid I had been.

"Bo, stay here!" I cried, taking off in a run.

Bo's voice jumped an octave. "Boss man, where are you going? How am I supposed to fight this thing?"

Still, the spear roared at me angrily from the roof. It did not move.

"It doesn't want us!" I cried, throwing open one of the doors to the pancake house and running inside. "Stay with Harris!"

The delightful smell of bacon, eggs, and ham hit me hard as I tore into the cozy, cedar-paneled foyer. A hostess was punching a credit card number into a terminal, and an elderly man was reaching for a toothpick as he waited for her. Both were frozen.

I blew past the front desk and slid to a stop on the tile floor. I looked around the dining room. The place was packed yet quiet as a catacomb.

Families were stuck in conversation. Diners were frozen in mid-chew. Waiters stood like statues with trays full of food.

I spotted the yellow shape I had seen from outside. Shoes scuffed across the floor and then a female voice cried, "Shit!"

A hooded woman in an amber puffer jacket broke for the kitchen. I wove around the dining room floor and took off after her.

I slipped under a busboy cleaning a table, grabbing a dirty plate covered in bacon grease off the table. I aimed it and chucked it with a forceful overhead throw. It shattered against the wall, narrowly missing.

The hooded woman glanced back as she spun around a cook flipping a pancake. She was a comet of yellow light.

I ran into the kitchen. I was gaining on her.

I grabbed a clean plate off a plate warmer and threw it.

CRASH!

The hooded woman ducked just before it connected against the wall. I cursed, tearing deeper into the kitchen.

The back door was near. I only had one more chance before she got away.

I swiped a food tray off the counter. I took a deep breath and launched it.

THWACK!

It hit her in the small of her back, making her stumble forward. She kept running.

I closed the gap and leaped. I landed on her just as she touched the push bar to the back door.

The door banged open, and we tumbled down two steps before smashing on gravel.

We struggled on the ground for a few seconds. The woman tried to push me away, but I pinned an arm down. A few strands of chestnut hair escaped from the hood, but she kept her face away from my gaze. The woman's other arm flew up in a fist that clocked me square in the jaw.

I let go, crying out in pain. I grabbed the collar of her puffer jacket in desperation.

Something snapped and jingled before tumbling to the ground and shattering.

"Double shit!"

Colorful glass lay at our feet—as well as the black metallic outline of a grasshopper frame that held it. Next to it, a photograph of two people—a man and a woman. The man was lying on a hospital bed, and the woman had her arms around him.

The woman gave me a hard push to the chest. I stumbled back.

The air exploded as if it had been pregnant with sound. Suddenly, time resumed and the great sound block disappeared. We were surrounded by the chirping of birds, the whirring of car engines, and the chill of a wintry breeze.

The curtain over the sun was yanked aside. On the sloped roof, the spear of light howled at the blue sky and dissolved into a mixture of yellow smoke and rain that spilled over the shingles.

My eyes widened at the sight just before another punch flew at me.

I ducked and narrowly missed the fist, but I lost my balance. I fell back into the gravel as the woman bolted across the parking lot.

I took off for her again, ready to dash across traffic as I reached the street. A semi honked at me. I stopped just before it breezed past. Seconds later, the woman was safely across the street, running through another parking lot, impossibly far away. She disappeared behind a hardware store.

I stared after her, hunched over and trying to catch my breath.

Before all of this crap started, I was prepared to stay out of this supernatural affair.

But now, Natkaal was going to have to deal with me—and he wasn't going to like it.

CHAPTER SEVEN

Our boyish detective was in bad shape after the encounter. The strange spear of light had disintegrated his car too.

Bo and I rushed Harris to the emergency room and sat in the waiting room as the nurses and doctors ran X-rays and patched him up.

If you want to get sick, go to a hospital. Everyone in the white-walled waiting room was either coughing up phlegm or wiping a runny nose. The unmistakable smell of "sneeze" was in the air. I was going to catch something if I stayed in here much longer, but I couldn't abandon Harris.

Harris had saved my life before. I simply returned the favor. If it hadn't been for me, the spear would have surely killed him.

Bo read a tabloid magazine while I stared emptily at a talk show playing on the TV in the corner, thinking about Natkaal. Nearby, a man yelled at the top of his lungs that he was sick, sick, sick and tired of waiting for hours in this place. Naturally, the nurses ignored him.

I had kept the broken suncatcher and some of the stained-glass shards. I examined them, trying to fit the shards into the metal grasshopper frame that had held them. They were irreparably shattered.

I also kept the photo the woman in the amber puffer jacket had dropped. I had more time to study it now. She had long, curly chestnut hair and wore a St. Louis Cardinals jersey. She looked late thirties or early forties, with piercing brown eyes. She wore tasteful makeup that covered her tanned face, with a layer of dark mascara and slightly rouged cheeks. Her smile was cheerful. She was not at all the kind of woman you thought would be a necromancer. But then again, necromancers never had a "stock" look. After all, look at me.

She huddled next to a man on a hospital bed. Had to be her husband. He was a man on chemotherapy, and judging from his sallow skin, he didn't have much time left. He lay in a hospital bed, smiling weakly.

I knew the tired, helpless look in her eyes. The look that betrayed that she knew her husband was going to die, but she didn't want the world to know that she knew. You're trying as hard as you can to hold it together, to get through every day. It makes you numb until one day you aren't. The emotions come in irregular waves. One minute, you're bringing your wife water in her bed as she recovers; the next, you're in your Lincoln Town Car, crying like a baby.

I guess you could say that photo dredged up emotions I hadn't felt in a long time. Whoever this woman was, I could relate to her.

But I had been here before. I knew how this movie ended. An amateur necromancer ventures into the dark art to save the person she loves. A demon double-crosses her. All hell breaks loose. Sound familiar?

You know who else knew this story and how it ended?

Natkaal…

A pneumatic door hissed open and a nurse walked out quickly, a stethoscope swinging around her neck.

"Lester and Bo," she called.

Bo and I looked at each other as the nurse motioned us to follow.

“Damian asked for you two,” the nurse said as the door closed behind us. We followed her down a bright, cramped corridor with a polished white floor, past curtained rooms to the end of the hall, where she parted a cobalt blue curtain, revealing Harris sitting on the edge of a hospital bed in an aseptic room.

The doctors couldn't hold him. He wasn’t bleeding, just bruised. He’d taken a hard hit on his chest and shoulders from where the spear lashed him. He was lucky to get away with no broken bones or internal organ damage. Despite copious painkillers and strict orders to take it easy, Harris was finessing his tie, primed for action.

Bo and I stared at him incredulously.

"You're crazy, you know that?" I asked.

Harris winced as he slid into his suit coat. "Not as crazy as you." He waited until the nurse left us. “You’re the one who jumped in front of the burning spear, remember?”

Bo scratched his head. “So, uh, what exactly did you tell the doctors, man?”

Harris rotated his arm and touched his shoulder gingerly.

“I told them I didn’t recall what happened,” Harris said. “Pissed the nurses off, but they know me around here. I told them I was on duty, and that’s all they needed to know. They know I’m with the force, and as long as I don’t have drugs in my system, they can’t argue with me.”

“The unexpected benefits of the golden badge,” I said.

“Speaking of unexpected benefits,” Harris said, “one of my colleagues gave me a ring. He’s assigned to Orman Misterka.”

I had forgotten about the gangly man for a while. Fighting a supernatural force will do that do you.

“After you called me about Misterka, I called my contact to see what I could find out,” Harris said. “He texted me while we were chatting in the pancake house parking lot. I couldn't answer for obvious reasons. Let's see if we can visit Mr. Misterka while we're here."

The ICU was in a separate wing of the hospital. Harris's badge got us in. Paintings of flowers adorned the walls, probably to provide peace to families while waiting on the mocha-colored couches—a big upgrade from the ER's stiff-backed chairs.

Harris crinkled a ten-dollar bill from his wallet and told me to get him a cold bottle of water and something for us. We left him leaning over the counter and joking with one of the nurses as he worked his charm.

The ICU vending machines were out of service. We found a humming vending machine in a shallow canteen outside Oncology. The canteen had a long laminate counter with a wicker basket full courtesy coffee pods and plastic silverware, a table with two chairs, and a vending machine full of colorful soda and water bottles.

Bo slipped the bill into the machine and punched some numbers. A few seconds later, three shiny water bottles tumbled into the bin, and I wrapped my fingers around their cool plastic shells.

"There go two of my favorite people," a female voice said. A tangle of long platinum hair drew my eyes to the corner of the little canteen.

My friend CeCe sat on a counter next to a coffee pod machine, arms folded as she grinned at us. Her couture red dress flowed over the counter like a waterfall of fabric. Amid the rush of red were two pale, bare feet.

She startled me. I smiled and clutched my heart. "Bad day to surprise me like that."

CeCe was a lich, a warden of the underworld. She was my

partner in crime as a necromancer before she died and ascended to her supernatural post. She had a habit of showing up unannounced. Trust me, she was a good person to have around on a day like this. Between her supernatural prowess and her sword, she was good backup in battle.

"Let me guess," I said. "You're here because word got 'round in the spirit world about the fight I just had."

A sarcastic grin spread across her pale face. The bad fluorescent lighting in this hospital made her look one hundred percent dead.

"What makes you think you're such a big deal down there?" she asked.

"Because Lester has friends in low places, remember?" Bo said, grinning.

"Your track suit is making me hungry," CeCe said.

"You like it, baby? Let me twirl around so you can see it better. Thrift store special."

"Looks like ketchup and mustard," CeCe said flatly.

"That's cold."

"The truth is cold, Bo."

Bo let out a loud belly laugh that carried down the hospital corridor. "A'ight. Next time, I'll wear purple for you."

"Okay, maybe I did hear about your scuffle," CeCe said, hopping down. "And maybe you are somewhat famous in the spirit world."

"CeCe, what the hell is Natkaal up to?" I asked.

"Making my life miserable, that's what."

She held a hand over the vending machine. The glass frosted over and turned into a low-fidelity screen with a living, moving parchment background. A highly accurate colored pencil drawing of Natkaal appeared, grinning against the parchment. His blood-red eyes burned with malice. His image pulsed on the parchment as if colored pencils were drawing him in real time.

"Once Natkaal's soul curse was lifted, he returned to his

normal self, something he hadn't been in over two hundred years," CeCe said.

Natkaal's mosaicked wings buzzed, and the grasshopper bounded into the air. The human hands under his thorax bloomed swords and sliced outward. Blood spurted from the swords, and dozens of insect demons spilled from the edges of the screen, screaming and gathering in a bloody pile. Caterpillars, spiders, beetles—all ugly monstrosities with human appendages attached. Natkaal's wings buzzed again as he landed atop the pile. He let out his bone-chilling horse whinny laugh.

"He went on a killing spree to establish his dominance," CeCe said. "He killed other demons for the pure joy of it. Before long, most demons went into hiding. Not even the strongest opposed him."

"But why?" I asked.

"Rumors are that he's using strange magic," CeCe said. "We don't know for sure. Whatever it is, it has the rest of the demon race pledging allegiance to him."

Atop the pile of dead demons, Natkaal laughed again.

"Can't the liches do something about it?" Bo asked.

"We don't interfere in disputes," CeCe said. "If demons want to wipe themselves out, it's not our concern."

"Then why is he making your life miserable?" I asked.

CeCe sighed as a bullhorn traced itself into one of Natkaal's human hands.

"Your Majesty!" he cried. "I request an audience. I declare a new kingdom of darkness; you and I are equal now. Acknowledge my power!"

He took flight and flew in circles around the parchment. "Or are you too chicken to witness my strength?"

Bo laughed. "Arrogant much, dog?"

"If you do not show yourself, I will take your kingdom," Natkaal said into the bullhorn.

"He's been looking for Halgeron," CeCe said as Natkaal buzzed in circles around the parchment.

"Looking?" I asked, picking up on her words.

Halgeron was the Lich King. The giant skeleton king was enigmatic, but not elusive—especially not to his subjects.

"Natkaal can't find him," CeCe said. "And neither can the liches or reapers. Halgeron has disappeared, Lester."

"How does the Lich King just disappear?" I asked.

"I came to warn you," CeCe said. "The liches are looking for him everywhere. We've been searching so much that our lakes of souls are neglected. We have closed them until further notice, so I'm afraid that séances are out of the question. It's a matter of security. We'll be leaderless if Natkaal starts a war with the liches."

"A war is exactly what we don't need," I said.

"Lester, if war breaks out, we'll have to recruit the reapers to help us. And if that happens…"

Reapers harvested the souls of the dead and transferred them to liches, who watched over them as they underwent a transformation into their next state.

"If there aren't any reapers, there will be fugitive souls," I said.

"And the dead will be among the living," Bo said. "Damn. Where's old Halgy when you need him?"

"Halgeron can stop a war," CeCe said. "But he picked a wonderful time to disappear."

Atop the dead demon pile, Natkaal snickered.

"Watch your back, Lester," CeCe said.

"You put the word out on the supernatural street that I won't let Natkaal start this war," I said.

CeCe put a hand on my shoulder and smiled. "Deal."

Somewhere, a loudspeaker announced a code blue, whatever that meant. Bo and I looked down the hall.

When I turned around, CeCe was gone.

~

Harris had come looking for us.

"I asked you guys to get me a bottle of water, not go on a pilgrimage," he said.

I shrugged. "Let's just say we had a supernatural rendezvous with a being of the sword-wielding, platinum-haired variety."

Harris nodded in understanding. "Did CeCe—"

A doctor in scrubs and a stethoscope around his neck wandered by, staring at his phone. Judging by his gait, he was probably on break.

Harris eyed him and stopped speaking immediately. When the man was safely out of earshot, he brought Bo and me close. Then, Harris eyed my shoulder and recoiled. "Yikes, man."

"That's not what I thought you were going to say," I said, remembering my conversation with CeCe.

Then I felt crawling little legs pricking against the shoulder of my coat.

A chocolate brown cockroach was scurrying across. It stopped for a moment, its antennae waving at me. Its brown shell was tank-like. I nearly jumped out of my skin as Harris knocked it off with the back of his hand.

"Motherjunker, you're asking for a funeral!" Bo cried. His face went warrior as he jumped into the air, aiming his feet at the roach.

WHAM!

Bo landed just next to the cockroach and missed. I could've sworn the ground shook as the dead man wobbled, slightly stunned.

"Get back here!" he cried.

The roach took off like a NASCAR racer; it disappeared under a baseboard.

"They're breeding like rabbits," Bo said.

"Like cockroaches," I corrected.

We stared at the baseboard for a moment, hoping the roach might scamper out for round two. It did not.

Harris brought us in close again.

"Anyway, I got the status on Misterka. It's bad. A concussion, cervical fracture, broken elbow, broken leg, a bruised lung, and cuts and scrapes all over. He required surgery immediately upon arriving at the ER."

"Damn," Bo said, wincing.

"My colleagues are having a tough time locating his family. We can't find any next of kin, and the only potential relative is a Kathleen Misterka, but our records show she no longer lives in St. Louis. She's in Colorado Springs, and she's not returning our phone calls."

"Probably divorced," Bo said.

"Is Misterka in stable condition?" I asked. "When might you be able to ask him?"

Harris sighed and put a hand on my shoulder. "I like the way you think, Lester, but that's the biggest problem of all. There was a complication during surgery. Orman Misterka is dead."

CHAPTER EIGHT

THE NEWS HIT me like a sledgehammer.

I needed to catch my breath. I needed to sit down.

"It's all right, boss man," Bo said, trying to console me in his softest voice. "It's all right."

I leaned against the wall, closing my eyes, blocking out the bright fluorescent lights, white walls, and endless corridors.

Orman Misterka was dead. And he died at *my* home. I tapped the wall gently.

"I'm sorry," Harris said. "It's a streak of damned bad luck, Lester. This sort of thing happens, though. It's not your fault."

A tear jumped into the corner of my eye as I thought about Misterka's family, even though the police couldn't locate them.

"I can't believe it," Bo said. "I just can't believe it."

The dead man snapped his fingers. "I didn't make that man fall down the stairs, but I gave him some bad juju. May the liches marinate my soul 100 extra years because of this."

Harris said some more kind words to me before one of the nurses motioned to him. He excused himself.

Bo and I took a walk. We passed through the long corridors without saying a word. I just needed to clear my mind.

You wouldn't believe how many twists and turns this hospital had. We ended up somewhere between Psychiatry and Cardiology when a pneumatic door opened and the hallway filled with chattering and hurried footsteps.

Two nurses pushed a gurney, surrounded by frantic doctors. They were headed right toward us.

"Out of the way, gentlemen!" one of the nurses cried.

The hallway wasn't wide enough for all of us. Bo and I freaked out and jumped to the side, but we still weren't out of the way.

Instinctively, I reached for a door nearby that looked like a restroom. We ducked inside as the gurney zipped by—on it lay an elderly man in an oxygen mask and a far-gone gaze.

Then the door shut, ushering in darkness for a moment.

"I thought this was the bathroom," Bo said.

We stood in front of a felt wall. Something drew me deeper into the shadows as my eyes adjusted to the minimal light. The air had a hint of something sour that I couldn't place—like mold or lingering body odor. The wall curved deeper inward to a single ray of orange light flecked with dust motes.

We wound around the felt wall. The room opened into a small chapel with a few modest wooden pews and an arched stained-glass window that was at least two stories tall. The window bathed the room in kaleidoscopic splendor as the sun shone through. High above, a giant troffer glowed like a luminous moon, emitting a soft white, ambient radiance downward.

I couldn't help but marvel at the stained glass. It was a mosaic of blue, orange, red, and green trefoils patterned to paint the room in calm, peaceful light. Most stained-glass images were religious; this one was like art on the back of a cereal box where you had to stare at it for a while before you saw anything, if you saw anything at all. All I could see were swashes of color and glowing trefoils.

I found myself unable to say much as I slid into a pew that faced a small lectern. I had been in the hospital chapel before when my wife was here, but not this one.

Bo sat next to me.

I pulled the grasshopper suncatcher from my coat and held it up to the light. I imagined the prismatic wall breathing light into the metal frame, replacing the glass.

"In periods of antiquity, churches used stained glass to show the sublime beauty of God," I said, angling the frame to catch a little more orange light. "It's said that every stained-glass window tells a story."

Bo folded his arms and tilted his head at the window. "And what's this one telling you?"

I stared at the arched window again, this time at a splotch of orange, blue, and purple glass. I shook my head.

A female voice spoke to us. "From the dark depths, light."

A black woman in ponytail dreads and ruby stud earrings sat in one of the pews. Bo and I hadn't seen her. She wore a beige business jacket with a white turtleneck. She must have been the chaplain. She smiled at us warmly. "At least, that's what I'm picking up."

I nodded to her. A few seconds later, she was sitting next to us.

"This window usually has a stupefying effect on people," she said. "It takes their mind off the unpleasant circumstances that brought them here. And that is enough."

"All the best to you and your family," Bo said. He clearly missed the memo that she was the chaplain.

The red-earringed woman gave him a half nod.

"They say that light heals," she said. "But it's also capable of evoking pain. When we shine light on the things that disturb us most, we must then face them. But if there is too much light, we cannot see. What matters is that we find the way between."

"Huh," Bo said, scrunching up his face. "Yeah, I guess."

"It's okay," she said. "The meaning will come to you when you need it."

"Oh," Bo said, even more confused. "Cool."

The woman stood, washed in the light from the arched window. The light rays gave her dreads a multichromatic lens flare, like the old cameras in the '70s used to do when you pointed them at someone standing in the sun.

"You two look like you're in need," she said. "Can we do anything for you?"

It was just her in the room. Speaking in the royal "we" didn't seem necessary, but hey, I wasn't going to correct her English.

But I knew what she was asking. I wasn't sure whether prayer would even help a guy like me anymore. I was so far into the dark art that I had resigned myself to my fate, whatever the big man upstairs had in store for me. All I knew was that I was doing my best, living by a good code, and helping people. When this is all over, when my world goes dark—I want to be buried in an unmarked grave. I want the Director of the St. Louis Grim Reaper Society to personally escort me to the spirit world. I want CeCe to be my lich, and I want to marinate with my family in lich water for as long as it takes to draw out my solace and atonement so I can move on to whatever the next plane of existence is. At least, that's how I have it worked out in my head.

The woman smiled at me. The wall picked up the rubies in her ears and made them wink.

"Can we do anything?" she asked again, pulling me from my thoughts.

"Thanks, but we're okay," I said, smiling back. "We didn't mean to disturb you."

"It is I who should be apologizing to you," the woman said.

"Well, we *are* looking for our way back to the ICU," Bo said.

"Down the hall and to the right," she said, pointing. "Right again, and then left. It's like a labyrinth in here sometimes."

We left her marveling at the brilliant stained-glass mural, her beige business jacket absorbing the light so that she herself looked part of the wall.

I gave her a lingering gaze before shutting the door quietly behind me.

CHAPTER NINE

PERHAPS AGAINST MY BETTER JUDGMENT, I invited Harris to stay with Bo and me for a few days. Whatever the supernatural force we encountered at the pancake house was, it wanted him dead. It had no interest in harming Bo and me. Plus, I had wizard-grade wards installed in my home, and Bo had a giant pot of soup that would warm the soul.

We swung by Harris's apartment so he could get a change of clothes for a few days. He lived in a brick apartment complex a few minutes west of downtown.

"So this is where the legend lives," Bo said, sliding into a parking space in front of the three-story building. It looked like it had been built around the turn of the twentieth century. The brick color scheme matched the impending sunrise, and the steel mansard roof reflected the late afternoon sun.

The building, while old, was cozy and carpeted. Harris checked his mail in the lobby, clanging his steel mailbox open and shut as Bo and I watched rays of sunlight stream in through a circular window high on the wall.

We followed Harris up a narrow stairwell to the third floor. Bo teased Harris about having a bachelor pad; Harris clapped back about Bo's ketchup and mustard tracksuit and how it looked like it belonged on a hot dog. I tried playing referee, but these two were in their element tonight—the painkillers had given Harris a new wind, and Bo was feeding off his energy. We laughed all the way down the hallway until we reached Harris's door.

It was cracked open.

Harris held out an arm, keeping both of us back. He shushed us immediately.

I wish I had brought the pistol that Bo and I kept in the glove compartment of my Town Car, but we had let our guard down. I cursed.

In a flash, Harris's service weapon was in his hand and pointed at the door.

Bo and I hung back as the boyish detective silently toed the door open with his dress shoe and led into the apartment with his gun first. Then, the apartment swallowed him.

Every second was like ten, every ten like a minute.

Bo and I waited with bated breath, expecting a gunshot or scuffle.

All was quiet.

An eternity later, Harris emerged, glancing suspiciously up and down the hallway. He was visibly rattled. He told us to wait again as he cleared the stairwell on the opposite end of the building.

"That's a great way to start the night," he said, holstering his gun as he returned.

He motioned us into the apartment.

Harris's apartment *was* a bachelor pad. You could tell only a man lived here. There was a glass coffee table that looked suspiciously like the one everyone had in their homes in the late 90s. Worn philosophy books were stacked neatly next to a remote. Terence McKenna, Jean-Paul Sartre, and Plato.

There was a lone coffee maker in the kitchen, and like many bachelor pads, not a single piece of art on the wall. The place needed a touch from the fairer sex, and that's being kind. But it was clean and simple. The furnace cycled on with a rush of toasty air, swaying the vertical blinds in front of his balcony.

The place looked...untouched. At least, there was nothing broken or ransacked. The last time someone broke into my house, it took me days to clean up the aftermath.

"What did they do?" I asked.

"What did they take is a better question," Bo said, slipping off his sunglasses and surveying the apartment. "They didn't take none of your books, did they?"

Bo grabbed a Terence McKenna book off the coffee table and thumbed through it, making a fish mouth. "You don’t strike me as the type that’s into psychedelics,” he said. “I'm learning more and more about you every day, Harris."

Any levity that Harris had had before discovering his apartment had been broken into was gone. His face was disturbed now, unnerved.

“There was nothing taken from what I can tell," Harris said.

I wandered across Harris's living room and into his kitchen with a discerning eye. I spotted something white on the counter.

An envelope.

The name *Det. Damian Harris* was written on the envelope in neat, feminine handwriting.

"Harris, you got a girlfriend?" I asked, not taking my eyes off the envelope.

"Not at the moment."

"Then you've got mail," I said, handing him the envelope. The boyish detective's eyes widened. At first, he thought it was a joke.

Bo and I watched with curiosity and trepidation as he produced a letter opener from one of his kitchen drawers, sliced open the top of the envelope, and produced a perfectly folded letter written on spiral notebook paper. His eyes darted left and right as he read the letter. His jaw dropped, and he looked up at me, speechless.

I took the letter and read it out loud.

The handwriting was definitely feminine. Cursive. The author had a proper education because they didn't teach cursive in public school anymore. The letters flowed across the lines like a work of art—not quite calligraphy, but beautiful to look at all the same. The pleasant appearance made it hard to believe what came next.

Detective Harris,

I hope this letter finds you in a speedy recovery. It was not my intention to cause you mortal harm, though it was my intention to hurt you.

My understanding of the Paranormal Crimes Division is that it consists of one man and one man only: you. Therefore, I write this letter to appeal to your character and reasoning.

Mr. Harris, I find myself at a crossroads in my life. I don't know which way is the right way. Surely when you were an amateur necromancer, you understood this problem—the push and pull to figure out just how many pieces there are to this art. Just how many ways there are to get into trouble.

You've taken a stand in the battle against right versus wrong, justice versus injustice, and righteousness versus the dark heart of malice. However, I don't see the world that way. There are journeys, and depending on the day and the alliance, the same decision could be right, wrong, moral, immoral, righteous, malicious, or somewhere between all of these. It doesn't mean that the actor is good or evil—it just means they're doing the best they can. Aren't we all doing that, Detective Harris?

I truly am doing the best I can. However, the death you are investigating has put me in the wrong light. I can assure you, and you must take my word that no crimes have been committed thus far. I intend to keep it that way, and if I am successful, you will never, ever hear from me again.

But I need you to drop your current investigation. It was a supernatural sacrifice, Detective Harris. No foul play.

There, I've solved the mystery. I'm sure there are plenty more supernatural crimes that will require your skills and intelligence. I ask that you divert your attention accordingly.

However (and this is where I appeal to your logic), I know it's not in your nature to do that. Should you continue your investigation of the man in the apartment, and should your investigation lead you to me, please be advised that I will have no choice but to deal you mortal harm.

It's not personal, but nothing gets in the way of love.

I truly wish you the speediest of recoveries.

Ever yours,

K

We stood in silence, fathoming what we just read.

"Get better soon, but stop the investigation or yo' ass is finished," Bo said. "She could have just given us the executive summary."

Harris frowned. "Sounds like we've got an even bigger problem on our hands than we thought."

CHAPTER TEN

My mother always taught me to keep the house clean because you never knew who would show up. I've had a thing about cleaning ever since. Keeping a clean house also helped me keep my mom's memory alive. As you get older, rituals become more important, especially those you learned from loved ones who have passed on.

I cleaned my bathrooms twice a week even when they didn't need it. When I went to the grocery store, I always bought some extra nonperishable food and snacks just because, including a six-pack of beer, a box of tea, and a bag of coffee. The way I was raised, you never knew when you needed to entertain a family member or friend, and it was bad form to get caught without extra provisions.

Bo's parents raised him right too. The dead man could do some serious damage with a bottle of disinfectant and a dish rag. You ought to see him with a feather wand too. He'd make Martha Stewart proud. As a result, my house was (usually) always ready for the coming of the good Lord himself.

My mother's training prepared me exactly for Harris to sleep over. The guy had just been injured and threatened with death, after all. He needed some hospitality.

I gave him the guest room on the third floor. It was spacious and big enough to fit three Harrises comfortably. With cherry hardwood floors polished to a high gloss, a mix of wainscoting and floral wallpaper, and corner slants where the ceiling met the roof, it had a lot of character. Plus, it had a great view of the sunrise and sunset.

"You're making me feel like a king," he said as I handed him a stack of freshly laundered towels and wash cloths.

"You're a guest," I said. "This place has wizard-grade wards, and my gang of undead spiders will detect a threat early. You need anything at all, just holler. Seeing as that golden spear didn't want to harm me, you should be safe here."

I could tell that Harris was touched. He thanked me, and I left him to change and freshen up.

Bo must've read my mind, because the spicy aroma of his delicious Tabasco chicken noodle soup hit me as I jogged down my back steps and into the kitchen. I didn't just want a bowl. I wanted two.

Bo was stirring the pot.

"There's one thing I can't figure out," he said, ladling soup into a ceramic bowl. "That spear wouldn't attack you or me."

I thought back to the fight. Apparently, there was something indelectable about the two of us that it didn't want to make us its next meal.

"And the letter from that chick—Kay, wasn't it? She didn't even mention us. It was like we didn't exist."

"We aren't the center of the supernatural world," I said as Bo set the steaming bowl of soup in front of me along with a lime wedge so ripe, it made my eyes water.

"Natkaal is behind this," Bo said.

"We know he's involved," I said, spooning into the bowl. Good God, the soup was even better than it was this morning.

Bo pointed the soup ladle at me. "If you die, Natkaal dies."

"And vice versa."

I didn't need to be reminded of the fact that Natkaal's blood flowed through my veins. After a vampire bested me in battle, a blood transfusion from the grasshopper demon saved my life—a gift from said vampire that defeated me. It was a sick joke, one that I would never forgive her for. Natkaal and I were interconnected for better or worse, and there wasn't a damn thing I could do about it. Trust me, the grasshopper didn't like it either.

"If everyone's favorite grasshopper demon didn't want to do mortal damage to himself, he would go out of his way to leave you untouched," Bo said.

Suddenly, the Tabasco chicken noodle soup didn't taste so good.

"You really think so?" I asked.

Maybe Bo had a point, but there were still too many facts that didn't add up. "Maybe Natkaal got into this Kay chick's head, just like Visgaroth did with you," he said.

I remembered my own suborning so many years ago from the scorpion demon Visgaroth who betrayed me, killed my wife and son, and robbed me of all the joy in my life up until that point. I spent seven years in atonement, swearing that I would never touch the dark art ever again. It made me sick to think that this amateur necromancer—whoever she was—was headed for the same path. Natkaal knew my story; maybe all of this wasn't a coincidence.

The thought of it all stressed me out. I did the only thing I knew how when I felt stressed. I reached over to the counter and switched on my little black stereo. An electric violin and shimmering synthesizers hummed out, filling the kitchen with the jazz of Jean-Luc Ponty. Bo pursed his lips and put a lid on the soup pot.

I needed a mind-expander right now. Something to disrupt my current thought patterns and take me to a different state. Jazz always did that. It was more intoxicating for me than alcohol—the chord runs, solos, and moods of the electric violin were as if Jean-Luc were speaking to me.

The back steps creaked, and before long, Harris emerged in a flannel shirt, jeans, and bare feet. He looked in pain, but he also looked hungry.

"Come and get you something to eat," Bo said, setting another bowl of Tabasco chicken noodle soup at the seat next to me.

“Jazz, eh?” Harris asked.

I nodded, listening intently to a guitar solo.

Harris rubbed his palms together. His eyes closed with delight as he savored the first mouthful. Then, after he licked a drop of soup from his lips, he said, "Seriously, which store brand is this?"

Without skipping a beat, Bo said, "It's from a little-known brand called Yo Mama."

"That's wrong," Harris said, laughing.

We ate in silence for a moment surrounded by jazz. After a while, I said, "Say, Harris, what do you think about all of this?"

I told him what Bo thought, about Natkaal being behind all of this, and why the spear of light didn’t attack me.

"Bo’s hypothesis isn't far off,” the boyish detective said. "But there's still the problem of the murder and the suncatcher.”

I had forgotten about the suncatcher in my pocket. I knew deep down somewhere in my heart of hearts that it held the key to Natkaal’s plans.

A crystalline synthesizer hit a minor seventh chord, and it got me thinking about darkness and wonder, like those chords always do, and how they often made me hold two dueling emotions in my heart at the same time.

“Harris, didn’t the murder victim have a suncatcher in his hand?”

“It’s in evidence,” he said.

“But it was intact, right?”

“As far as I remember.”

“Can we get it?” I asked.

“You can see it, sure,” Harris said. “Tons of paperwork for me, though.”

“I want to know what’s so special about it,” I said.

I had an idea. I checked my watch.

“Where you going, boss man?” Bo asked.

“Away for a bit,” I said, swiping my winter coat off the hook next to the porch. I pulled out the suncatcher’s shell and held it up. “I’m going to educate myself on a few things."

CHAPTER ELEVEN

THERE ARE times when you just need to be alone. I needed to clear my mind.

I left Bo and Harris laughing in the kitchen. Bo knew what was up, and he was good about giving me space. Harris was on so many painkillers that I doubt he would've cared anyway. At least he was safe. I didn't need two houseguests dying on me in one day.

I took Hazel with me. She had been cooped up in the house all day and needed to get out. Her tail wagged uncontrollably as she followed me to the garage.

Hazel loved to go on car rides, especially when it was just me and her. It was too cold to let the window down and let her stick her head out with her tongue lolling as I cruised down the inner-city boulevards, so she sat at attention in the passenger seat as I eased my Lincoln Town Car out of the garage, down my loud, crunchy gravel alley, and into the world.

~

I signed up Hazel for service animal certification a few years ago. She's extremely well trained and no one would be able to tell otherwise. A quick website visit, a five-minute survey, and ten business days later, Hazel Broussard had her official service dog papers.

I did this so I could take her anywhere with me. It was unsafe to leave her in the car alone when it was this cold. Plus, gangs around here were notorious for kidnapping dogs and selling them into the dogfighting circuit. That happened to one of my neighbors a few years ago, and it broke my heart.

So sue me for signing Hazel up as a service dog.

I've only ever been challenged once. A mean department store manager insisted on knowing my medical condition upon seeing my paperwork. I told her I was a necromancer and that I had the power to control the dead. I also told her that my undead servant was parking my car and that he would be joining me shortly so I could buy him some drawers.

She didn't give me any more trouble after that.

Our first stop was the St. Louis Central Library. A stately, 20th-century marble and granite building downtown, it is one of the most beautiful libraries in the world and a hidden gem in the city. You know you're in the presence of masterful architecture when the first thing you do after you walk in the door is look up.

I found myself craning upward to gaze in wonder at the sleek marble walls lit with alcove lights and the Renaissance fresco on the ceiling, replete with clouds, sky, and portraits of poets.

Hazel sniffed the floor madly as we entered.

The library has a majestic arched stained-glass window with hues of blue, purple, white, and green. From afar, it makes you feel as if the narrow stairwell is undersea. Angular rays shine down like sunshine from the surface of the sea, and the colors on the window dazzle and dance like kelp. In Latin are the words "Poesis Musica."

Musical poetry.

Light has a music of its own. As I was finding, it also had its own poetry.

The stacks rose high around Hazel and me as we wandered down the aisles, taking in the irresistible woody, musty scent that often pervaded libraries.

I found three books and settled into a mahogany reading table in the Great Hall, surrounded by empty space, dying sunlight, and an occasional teenager studying at a table far, far away.

Hazel lay at my feet under the table as I studied the books.

"Within the hollowed interiors of cathedrals, the sun's rays imbued the stained glass with an ethereal glow, casting a kaleidoscope of vibrant hues upon the sacred ground. The warm caress of radiant light enveloped the beholder, inspiring awe and a sense of sanctity."

"Crimson as the wine of communion, blue as the heavens opened in revelation—the translucent glass sings its hymn of jeweled light. Gothic cathedrals rise with walls of illuminated scripture, saints showered in brilliant rays as they suffer. Each pane is a glittering sermon. Stained

glass brings these sacred stories to life in radiant color and symbol, ministering to the spirit through beauty sublime."

The books gave me a page full of detailed notes. I wrote until my hand cramped.

Hazel trotted behind me as I placed my leather-spined teachers on a return rack and waved at a librarian.

I folded the page of notes and tucked it into the interior pocket of my winter coat as I broke out into the wintry starlight. It's a good sign when you enter the library with the sun in the sky and emerge into a night full of stars.

I found a stick and played fetch with Hazel all the way to the car.

"It would be my pleasure to help you find stained-glass sheets that meet your needs," an aproned middle-aged woman said, gesturing me down aisles of resplendent, rainbow-colored stained glass. Somewhere, the distinctive buzz and hiss of a soldering iron underscored the quiet, colorful shop.

I followed her into a prismatic aisle. I had to stop Hazel from sniffing some sawdust on the floor.

A slanted skylight framed the woman as she slid out a forest green sheet of glass with a *shing*. The frosted glass reflected her face and distorted it before she poked her head out from one side.

"Will this color suit you?"

I nodded.

She pulled out several more colors, naming them as she clinked the pearlescent sheets together against the wall—cloister garden green, monk's robe brown, sacred fire orange, and dove wing white.

I set a soldering iron, steel brackets, and flat-lipped grozier pliers on a conveyor belt. They hummed toward a teenaged cashier with a mop of black hair who stared at them like a grocery store kid stares at fruits and vegetables they've never seen in their lives.

Nearby, the hardware store manager clicked off the "Open" sign in the front window and turned off the automatic doors. A voice came on the loudspeaker and asked customers to make their final selections. The store was closing in five minutes.

"Find everything okay?" the cashier asked. He glanced at Hazel. "Nice dog, by the way."

Hazel tilted her head, her tongue hanging out.

I took Hazel to a drive-through of a local coffee shop. We sat for an eon before the barista opened the window, filling my car with the aroma of delicious roasted coffee. She handed me the most important part of my order—not coffee, tea, or a designer drink, but a cup of whipped cream for Hazel. She made a baby voice at Hazel before handing me a black americano.

Hazel lapped up the whipped cream in seven seconds flat.

I knew enough about stained glass now—its history, uses, and ultimate purpose. Now I just needed the final piece to hold it all together.

That piece, you ask?

I parked in the alley and sent Hazel into the house. I pulled out my necromancy kit from my winter coat inside pocket. It was a leather kit with chalk, kids' birthday candles, and string.

I went to work, scrawling out two perfect concentric circles on my garage floor. Unlike the unfortunate man who lost his life in the apartment, my circles were professional necromancer-grade. There were no dented-in lines or slips of the wrist in my craft.

I drew my garage shades, lit the candles in the inner circle, and sat on a blanket in the outer circle.

Normally, I close my eyes when I state my intentions, but this time, I wanted to see every moment. I wanted to see every feature of the grasshopper's face when I ensnared him in my ritual.

I took a deep breath, exhaled, and called Natkaal.

CHAPTER TWELVE

All you have to know when calling the spirit world is a name. Names have immense power both in this world and in the great beyond. With a name, you invite and call upon an entire person's life. The good, the bad, and the ugly. You invite them to show themselves that they might help you in exchange for a favor.

How many times had I channeled the great beyond and tangoed with the things that go bump in the night? I lost count.

I *did* know how to count my grievances with Natkaal, though. Oh, let me count the ways.

"You who helped me slay Visgaroth."

I held the grasshopper's red eyes and his sinister smile of triangular teeth in my mind's eye.

"You whose blood flows through my veins like a strange river."

I imagined Natkaal hanging upside down from a thin strand of silk in my basement as my furnace blazed behind him.

"You who helped me hunt a silent spirit through the world of the living."

Now, the grasshopper was preening itself on the bottom branch of the maple tree in my backyard under the pale light of a waxing crescent.

"You who saved my grandson from a smothering death."

Natkaal held my grandson in his human arms now. He perched at the top of my stairs, half in shadow, half in waning transom sunlight as a group of gangbangers inched toward him, guns drawn.

"You who betrayed me."

My garage darkened. In the fading rays of natural light, two giant cockroaches scurried up the wall and into the rafters. I kept my eye on the inner circle.

A shadow bloomed in the rafters, materializing like flowing plasma. The light flowed—no, rippled over the walls like my garage was the underside of a wooden dock in moonlight. First, Natkaal's mosaicked wings separated from his body and flapped twice before angling into a resting position on his back. Two muscular, alabaster-colored human hands tugged on a strand of silk that appeared to weave itself out of nothingness. The giant springbox legs swung down, followed by a torpedo-shaped thorax. Then, the grasshopper met me face to upside-down face. The only thing that hadn't changed was his crazed, horse whinny laughter that shook the walls of the garage and threatened to blow me out of the circle.

"It has been a while, Lester."

"Not long enough," I said, my face hardening like stone.

Neither of us said anything for a while. Natkaal swayed on his silk strand and I stared him down, not blinking.

"This is the part where you tell me that I have a lot of explaining to do," Natkaal said, flipping right side up on the strand and landing in the inner circle with the grace of a ninja. "Followed by the part where I tell you that it's none of your business." His smile faded. "Are we done now?"

"What the hell are you up to?" I asked.

The demon opened his mouth to answer, but I held up a

hand. "Before you tell me it's none of my business, I'll remind you that I can be a supernatural pain in the ass."

Natkaal gave me a long face. "Lester, I know you better than you know yourself, better than you know your reality."

The comment took me off guard.

The grasshopper had struck a nerve and he knew it. "Nothing you have done has been done without my permission," Natkaal said. The grasshopper finally sat down and looked at his human nails like a teenage girl would. "Of course you would interfere. That is your way. Of course you would call me here for a meeting of the minds." He switched his eyes from his nails to my face, settling into a malicious grin. "You can't handle the truth."

Every bone in my body was on fire. If my hands were big enough, I would have reached into the inner circle, broken it, and ripped his head off his body. Instead, I yelled, "I don't care what it is—I won't let you get away with it!"

"You owe your existence to me!" Natkaal said. He brought his face to the edge of the inner circle and gnashed his teeth. "I left you out of this so that you could live your life, necromancer! And this is how you repay me?"

"That's what lack of loyalty gets you," I said. "You may not be loyal to anything, but I'm loyal to principles. When you were with me, I appreciated it. But now that we're on opposite sides, I won't have any mercy on you. You, Visgaroth, and all the other insect demons—you're no different to me now."

Natkaal let out a whinnied laugh. It settled between us for a few seconds.

"Things *are* different now," he said. "I regret that what happened happened, Lester. But we are in a new paradigm."

"That's a fancy word for you," I said.

"The real question is this: are you prepared to live the blues?"

"What kind of question is that?"

"You want to know what I'm up to, so I'll tell you,"

Natkaal said. "You're too corrupted, Lester. I need a necromancer I can mold, someone to do my bidding without asking questions."

"Like I did with Visgaroth," I said.

"No, *not* like you," the grasshopper said. "Your conscience went and awakened. That was always the problem with you. This isn't supposed to be a profession where your morals guide you. We're talking about the dark art of necromancy, after all."

Natkaal glanced around the garage, up into the rafters. "Just like I was never meant to be good, no necromancer was ever meant to be good either. I suppose that's what connects us, you and me. It is also what severs us. Such a pity that we are connected by blood. A real pity. If it weren't for fate, our two anomalies would have worked themselves out, don't you think?"

"So you believe in fate," I said.

"Only when it suits my purposes," Natkaal said. "And it is fated that this new entrant into the dark art will do as I say. She is smart, resourceful, and she will not quit. I have molded her to my liking. Try and corrupt her, Lester, but it will bring you only pain. Just as it did in the past."

Natkaal showed the open palms of his human hands. He was making an offering.

"Here is my proposition, and I'm not negotiating, necromancer. You stay out of my way, and I will stay out of yours."

"And if I don't?"

Natkaal sighed.

"You can't kill me," I said, grinning.

"No, I can't."

"I'll forever get in your way," I said. "I'm prepared to die for my principles. Are you?"

My words disturbed Natkaal. Every inch of his grasshopper face contorted into anger. His viridian exoskeleton darkened to a shade between viridian and black.

"You lie," he said.

"How about you fool around and find out?"

Natkaal had lost his breath. He hated every word I had said. I had stirred up an allergic reaction. Now I knew how to push *his* buttons.

The viridian color returned to his exoskeleton and he let out a derisive laugh—not his usual horse whinny, but a mocking laugh that started low and slow, then boomed around the garage.

"You are not ready to die," he said finally.

"And you thought you knew me," I said, clenching my fists. "I guess all your time among the living taught you nothing about humanity."

"You are ready to abandon Marlese?" Natkaal asked.

His words zapped the power from my clench. My fists slackened, went to sleep as if I had been sitting on them this entire time.

"And your grandson," the grasshopper said. "You're ready to let him grow up without a grandfather? What does that do to a child, I wonder, mmm?"

The words made me weak. Suddenly, I couldn't speak.

"I have my answer," he said, snarling. "And you have your warning."

A strange wind blew in the garage even though the door and windows were closed. Natkaal disappeared in a wisp of silvery blue smoke, and the candles flickering in the inner circle were snuffed out like after a small child blew on a birthday cake.

It got cold. Colder than the coldest wintry day.

Outside, starless moonlight cut across the garage, across my circle. I sat weak-kneed and unable to stop the tear from welling up in my eye, streaming down my cheek, and splashing to the floor.

CHAPTER THIRTEEN

THERE WAS no sleeping after my encounter with Natkaal, so I went to work. I needed to do something to take my mind off the conversation with the grasshopper. He had succeeded in rattling me.

Deep in my heart of hearts, I knew he was right. Maybe no one was ever truly ready to die, but I had a lot of life left to live. The thought of leaving Marlese and Malcolm made me numb, but so did the thought of letting Natkaal achieve his plans. Worse, there was no middle ground. The only way to forget about all of this was to absorb myself in work.

I have a shop in my garage. I'm a handy guy, and there's very little that stumps me in the way of construction. I learned from my dad, and this garage was his shop too. Between two generations of handy folks, you accumulate just about every tool you can imagine. I covered the walls with pegboards, and I had my tools neatly organized, ready for action at a moment's notice.

I swiped a compact tape measure and a glass cutter off the wall. The cutter belonged to my grandfather, who was the founder of one of the city's first black glazier unions. It had a golden knob on one end and a blade on the other, and it had real heft in my palm. I thought about my grandfather in that moment as I prepared the tools and laid out two sawhorses with a piece of ply board on top.

I worked out here a lot when my wife Amira was alive. It was a great way for me to get out of the house and just think —long before I dabbled in the dark art, long before I became the good necromancer I am today, I was just a humble handyman. I have fond memories of cutting all the baseboards for my house in here. I even replaced the trim on the door of my garage. There's a splotch of bunched-up concrete stuck to the floor from when I mixed a patch of cement for the back steps and got a little too zealous. Back in those days, there was nothing like getting lost in your work, following your fingers to solve a problem, and seeing the solution implemented by your own hands in front of your own eyes in living color to become part of the fabric of your home and family.

In this garage, I practiced the art of long-term vision: repairs I dreamed up in here for my home would last for half a century, maybe more. That was something to be proud of.

I laid out the sheets of stained glass on the plywood. I pulled out the metal frame of the grasshopper suncatcher and held it up against the light. I set it down on the sheets, angling it to get a sense of how the glass might look. I wanted something that would be the same size.

On a sheet of paper, I sketched an image in black permanent marker and trusted my instincts. I started with pointed ears—both standing at attention. Then I dragged the pen downward to a big head, dipped down for a lolling tongue that would be its own shard. Then, a big, muscular body that would require a few shards of brown.

Soon, Hazel was looking at me from the paper. At least, the best version of Hazel I could manage. I put her over the top of the grasshopper metal frame to compare the sizes. I was spot on. I cut out the shapes and placed them over the corresponding colors of glass, my marker squeaking over the glass as I drew outlines.

I scored the colorful sheets with the glass cutter and used the grozier pliers to nibble away at the edges. I worked slowly, dribbling finished glass shards onto the plywood.

I smiled. I still had the handyman's touch.

I used the metal fasteners, and a serpentine line of lead came to affix the glass shapes. I always thought it was strange that the metal was called "came." Never quite sounded right to the ear, but that's how you pronounced it. Because I was working with lead, I had to wear leather work gloves, protective eyewear, and a cloth mask for protection, and I had to keep the metal as far from my face as possible. I remembered I'd have to soak my equipment in sanitizer when this was all over and wash my hands thoroughly. Little things you learn and never forget.

Before long, I had a circular suncatcher that was as big as my palm. And instead of an evil grasshopper demon, I had the best counter I could think of—a loyal dog. Hazel sat smiling as the sun rose behind her. At least, that was what I tried to create. The reds and oranges behind her approximated a sunrise.

I soldered the pieces of glass to the metal fasteners and lead came. I finished by punching out a small hole in the glass for a metal chain to hang the suncatcher.

I must have lost track of time as I put my tools away and cleaned up. I pulled off my cloth mask and breathed a sigh of fresh air and relief.

Working with the glass had given me an idea to update one of the transoms on the second floor—the one to my room. I thought it would be beautiful if I covered the existing window with stained glass so that I woke up every morning in a color wash of sunlight.

With the suncatcher in hand reflecting the starlight, I yawned and stumbled my way back into the house. The kitchen was dark now, and only remnants of the spicy Tabasco chicken noodle soup aroma remained. Bo had cleaned up the stock pot; it hung on its place on the wall.

I washed my hands, put the suncatcher into a paper bag, and slipped quietly up the back steps. The hallway to my bedroom was bathed in blue and white streaks from starlight. The light was off in Bo's room just off the stairs. I peeked up the stairwell to the third floor. Harris's light was still on.

I'd be lying if I told you I wasn't thinking about Natkaal, but with the dog suncatcher resting on my nightstand, I felt some comfort that I was making progress, that I was finally doing something right, even though I didn't know what it was.

Somehow, a suncatcher was the key to all my problems. Now, maybe I had a key that would unlock some solutions. Call it intuition.

Hazel curled into a ball at the foot of my bed and gallivanted off to dreamland.

I wasn't far behind her.

CHAPTER FOURTEEN

Leave it to late winter to have an existential crisis. When I went to bed, it was colder than the dickens outside. When I woke up, the snow was melting. It wasn't warm enough to forgo my winter coat, but it was warm enough to qualify as a heat wave.

I called the attorney that Harris had found for me. He agreed to meet me on my porch in an hour. I guess that's what having good friends does for you.

The guy was a strapping young lawyer in a leather aviator jacket and white slacks. My spiders alerted me to him taking pictures of my front steps at every angle and distance.

"You don't have much to worry about, Mr. Broussard," he said, shaking my hand and introducing himself. "I've seen much worse. Your steps are fairly new. Best I can tell, they don't violate any codes or city ordinances."

"You're damn right they don't," I said. "I poured the cement myself and checked with a friend of mine who's an inspector for the city. Everything's in tip-top shape."

The attorney glanced down at a black scuff mark on one of the steps where the black shell case had fallen. "You said he was carrying a case, right?"

"That we offered to help him with twice," I added.

"It's pretty cut and dry," the man said, "but anything is possible. I don't think you'll be hearing from Mr. Misterka's family, but if you do, give me a call. I'll send these pictures to their attorney and give them a good chewing out—pro bono of course. You get the Damian Harris discount."

I shook his hand again. "Best discount in town."

The attorney jogged down the steps and stopped abruptly. He knelt. I watched curiously as he jammed a hand into the snow. He pulled up a golden, jingling blur.

"These yours?" he asked, dangling a key ring.

I glanced at the white cargo van still parked in front of my house.

"Mr. Misterka's," I said as the attorney handed the keys to me. I sighed at the fact that I'd probably have to give them to one of his family members. The keys were as cold as snow; there was a black key fob that sat in my palm like a malformed stone. I wondered if it still worked after being submerged in snow for so long.

I waved and stood on my porch as the lawyer drove off in his black Mercedes sedan.

A twist of light and a gray rippling caught the corner of my eye. I could've sworn I spied a liver-spotted hand correct the curtains in Granny's front window.

I pursed my lips as I returned to the house and threw Misterka's keys on my radiator in the foyer.

Bo wasn't one to cook when there were plenty of leftovers in the fridge, especially when the night before was one of his greatest hits. He brewed a pot of coffee and heated up his Tabasco chicken noodle soup on the stove. The kitchen smelled like hot sauce and Colombian blend, which was oddly pleasant and delicious.

Harris sat at the table reading the morning's newspaper—yes, I still subscribe to physical newspapers and no, I'll never read the online edition—and he was sipping a mug of coffee.

He was dressed in an immaculate suit he'd brought from his apartment. I was getting the feeling that if I ever saw Harris in a t-shirt, I'd probably need to report him to the psych ward.

"Arthur's a peach, isn't he?" the detective asked with a winsome smile.

"Told me exactly what I wanted to hear," I said.

"See?" Harris said. “You have nothing to worry about."

As soon as he finished speaking, the doorbell in the hall beat itself senseless with a clatter of buzzing and ringing.

I still had an old-fashioned, 20th-century bell, and there was no mistaking when someone was at the door. Given that my spiders didn't alert me, it had to be someone from my small VIP list…

It was Granny.

Through the peephole, I saw she had a plate covered in tinfoil and a big smile. She was dressed in a pearl necklace with a wooden rosary and a red floral dress that went down to her knees. A wall of petally, chemical perfume seeped through the door. Granny looked like she was ready for church, but it wasn't Sunday. That only meant one thing.

"I thought you could use some peach cobbler," she said, shoving the plate into my hand and inviting herself in.

"I appreciate the gesture," I said, "but we're—"

"Did I see you had company?" Granny asked.

I sighed with a smile as I followed Speed Racer into the kitchen.

She paused in the kitchen threshold with her hands on her hips, looking around slowly. She gave Bo a slow nod.

Bo jumped upon seeing her. "Good morning, Mrs. Powell," he said with a surprised frown.

Bo *never* called her Granny. I got the sense that if he did, she might have an allergic reaction. Anybody that wouldn't eat her cooking might as well have been dead to her. If only she knew the double entendre at play here.

"I thought I saw a handsome young man coming in and

out of the house," Granny said, settling on Harris. "And boy, when I'm right, I'm right. How you doin', baby? I'm Granny. You like peach cobbler?"

Harris grinned. "I ought to stay over at Lester's house more often."

Granny plopped down at the kitchen table next to Harris. "Don't say you *like* peach cobbler and not eat any, now," she said, giving Bo the side-eye.

Bo stirred the soup nervously, unsure what to do with himself.

Hazel trotted down the hallway and greeted Granny. The old woman took Hazel's face in her hands. "There's my good girl," she said. "You, Lester, and this handsome man will have to eat that *whole plate* of cobbler. You got that, Hazel?"

An irritated grunt emerged from the stove. Granny's words had hit Bo where it hurt. She sure wasn't being subtle today.

Granny turned to me. "What did that attorney say?" she asked. "I had my window cracked, but he didn't speak with conviction like lawyers should. I think you need to find another one."

I set the plate of peach cobbler on the table. I folded my arms and stared at her for a few seconds. "Granny, you're something else, you know that?"

The old woman frowned. "I'm following protocol, Lester Broussard. I didn't come empty-handed. You need peach cobbler like a plant needs sunshine because everybody needs peach cobbler and can't nobody tell me I'm wrong. And you *know* I go to my senior citizen center on Thursday mornings. The bus will be here to pick me up any minute. And you *know* that I only go up there but once a week. If I stroll in empty-handed with no gossip, the girls'll give me the cold shoulder. So spill the beans!"

When I didn't say anything, Granny glanced at Harris and tilted her head at me. "You see how he treats my hospitality? I never got your name, baby."

"Damian," Harris said, extending a hand. Granny took it as gently as a southern belle.

"Mr. Damian, one day you're gonna be old like me, and you're not gonna have any grandkids who want to visit you. You'll be sitting in your front room, watching soap operas all day, and your children—and your *neighbors*—will pretend like you don't exist. But when *they* need something—"

I threw up my hands. "Okay, okay. You win."

Granny shot me a sly smile.

"I ain't got all day."

I recapped the conversation with the attorney. Then I told her that Misterka was dead.

Granny let out an audible gasp. Her fingers went to the rosary around her neck and she uttered a short prayer. "Aren't you glad you called a lawyer?"

I thought about it for a moment. "You know, I am. You were right, Granny," I said in the singsong tone that I usually used when she was right about something.

"May the Lord keep his soul and keep *you* out of court."

She reached over and patted Harris's hand. "You come over more, you hear? I think I like you, Mr. Damian."

Bo was at the refrigerator now, fumbling with some food containers. He dropped one, and chicken noodle soup spilled on the floor and encroached on Granny's feet like slow-moving lava.

"Mmm mmm mmm," she said, glancing between Bo and the river of soup with disapproval. "You might want to clean that up."

Hazel started lapping up the soup. I reprimanded her and she stood down.

A metallic jingle spread across the kitchen. Granny pulled out her flip phone.

"What's up, dog?" she said in a dry tone.

She listened. "Early today again, Jaquan? Sometimes I think you're trying to win over my heart."

She flipped her phone shut. "If y'all'll excuse me, I got an appointment to chat with my girls and play a mean game of cribbage."

And like the whirlwind she had come in on, Granny was gone, closing my front door behind her as a diesel school bus purred on the street and honked at her.

"She's intense," Harris said.

"You don't even know the half of it," Bo whined. He was on his knees, soaking up the soup with a clump of paper towels.

"I get the sense she doesn't like you that much," Harris said with a smirk.

"Whatever gave you that impression?" I asked, swiping my coat off the hook. "I'll heat up the car."

Bo spread the paper towels over the floor, mumbling to himself.

"I'd pay money to eat that woman's peach cobbler if I could, but some things just can't be helped, man," the dead man said quietly to himself.

Harris chuckled. I didn't. Granny had taken it too far again, but I didn't have time to play referee today.

I had a suncatcher to look at.

CHAPTER FIFTEEN

The evidence room for the Paranormal Crimes Division was exactly what you would expect: a dark, climate-controlled room in a police station basement devoid of any natural light or accidental prying eyes.

Bo and I followed Harris into a cargo elevator with latticed gates. The car hummed downward two floors into a subbasement before jolting and dinging.

Halfway down a cool, breezy fluorescent-lit corridor with dark walls, we greeted an elderly black man behind a metal cage. He looked sleepy and as if he were going to retire any minute. Behind him, rows of neatly labeled office boxes were ranged on industrial metal shelves under harsh lights. A desk held some boxes for mid-processing. A knife, bloodstained shirt, and handgun in a sandwich bag were visible in one box.

I imagined all the smells a place like this held in its depths: the metallic tang of gun smoke, acridness of chemicals, and a hyper whiff of drugs – echoes of hundreds of crime scenes. Setting foot in here was yet another confirmation that being a paid police consultant wasn't why I was put on God's green earth. And the stuff I saw was just the *normal* crimes. I shuddered to think what untold paranormal wonders rested down here in nefarious slumber.

Harris gave the man a fist bump under the opening in the cage.

"Don't see you down here much, Harris," the man said. "Who'd you bring with you?"

The man gave us a brotherly nod, the kind that black people give when we mean strangers in our race well.

"Consultants," Harris said. "We should be all good on the permission front, right?"

The black man nodded. He had Harris sign a logbook and slipped Bo and me some legal papers to sign. "Yeah, the brass came down here and told me you needed something. I'm assuming it's related to that apartment murder, right?"

A moment later, the man slid us three pairs of latex gloves and an envelope with a bubble insert.

Harris put on the gloves and pulled out the grasshopper suncatcher. The photograph hadn't done it justice. I expected it to be muted in color, but in real life, it was as brilliant as any work of stained-glass art. Natkaal was depicted in glorious fashion, the glass around and within him gleaming like a glorious sunrise. The suncatcher was meticulously crafted, every shard perfectly placed. I wondered what hands conceived it.

Harris held the suncatcher up to the fluorescent light, and I couldn't help but think that the dismal lighting down here didn't do us any favors. I needed to know what this suncatcher did in sunlight, not the sickly fluorescent lights of an old police station basement.

"I need to get this outside," I said.

Harris glanced at the recordkeeper for permission.

The man waved. "As long as you folks need."

~

We stepped out into the lukewarm sunshine. Harris took us to a picnic table in the shade next to the police station. A giant sycamore gave us good cover, but the shade reminded me that we were definitely in the throes of winter. Occasionally, a squad car passed, followed by echoes of radio chatter.

Harris opened the envelope and brought the suncatcher into the light. The circular glass radiated so brightly that I had to look away.

Down in the dark basement, the glass was a masterpiece; here, in nature, it was a living, breathing show. Natkaal's mosaic grasshopper wings caught the light in bright twinkles. His red eye was crimson as blood.

I pulled out the broken suncatcher from the battle in the pancake house. I laid it on the picnic table next to the intact one. They were identical.

"We have two," I said, "but I wonder if these are the only ones."

From my pocket, I unrolled the paper bag and produced the suncatcher of Hazel. Now there were three.

A chill rustled the sycamore branches as we studied the three suncatchers.

"What else do you know about the man that died in the apartment?" I asked.

"Caucasian male, about 45 years old," Harris said. "But he's a John Doe. Lived in an apartment in the county. He had rented it for about three months, but he did it under an assumed name. The guy had no criminal record, so we can't find any other traces of him."

"Just three months?" I asked. "Let me see those pictures again."

Harris opened the envelope of pictures. I thumbed back to the dead man's hand with the suncatcher. I focused on a detail that I had overlooked—a dull gold wedding band on his ring finger.

I tapped the ring. “Our man is married. You didn’t find any evidence of a spouse?”

“Negative,” Harris said. "The whole thing is a mystery wrapped in an enigma, doused with Bo's famous Tabasco sauce."

"I resent you bringing my delicious soup into this mix," Bo said, wagging a finger at Harris. "But yeah, that's a pretty accurate description."

Suddenly, Bo's voice lost its natural echo. It escaped his mouth and then went flat halfway across the parking lot, like someone placed lead walls around the police station.

Every hair on my body stood on end as the sky darkened in sudden nightfall.

"Guys, she's back!" I cried.

Harris drew his service weapon. Nearby, a squad car was frozen on the street.

I gathered the suncatchers into the paper bag and evidence envelope and tucked them into my coat for protection. If my theory was right, they would be safe with me.

Bo balled his fists and said, "There she is. Back for round two."

A few yards away, the woman in the amber puffer jacket stood in the snow like a dead specter. I imagined violins shrieking as she stepped toward us.

Her hands went to her hood and she pulled it back, revealing long, curly auburn hair. Her green eyes were troubled—I imagined my eyes must've looked like that when I was under Visgaroth's control. She didn't have a villain's scowl or a madwoman's demeanor.

It was the woman from the photo.

"Playtime is over," she said. "Hand over the suncatcher."

CHAPTER SIXTEEN

Bo, Harris, and I didn't move. We just stared at the woman. She was a normal woman—not someone you would suspect of being involved in the paranormal. The puffer jacket gave her a decidedly tomboyish look.

Lightning sizzled in the blistering shadows that billowed around us.

"I won't ask you again," she said. "Hand it over."

I patted the paper bag on my chest. "You're not getting this until you explain what you're up to."

The woman took several steps toward us. Harris pointed his gun at her and yelled for her to stop. She obliged and shrugged.

"Whatever Natkaal is promising you, it won't turn out the way you think," I said. "He'll ruin your life. If you're unlucky, he'll take it from you."

I pulled out the photograph the woman had dropped and held it up high for her to see. "Your husband—is he why you're doing this?"

The woman stared at me blankly. I didn't know if he was her husband, but I had to try something. If I wanted info, I needed to rattle her. I charted the best possible path in my head and went with it.

"You can't bring him back," I said. "Trust me, I tried. Even if I had succeeded, it wouldn't have been the same."

The woman's mouth twitched just a little. I had guessed right.

"I know you don't want to listen to me," I said. "Nobody ever listens to me. But I've been here before. No amateur ever wants to accept that this could all go south. I worked with a young woman once who wanted to bring my son back. It didn't work. Then, I worked with an amateur couple who thought they could start a cult of demon summoners on the weekends. They're both soaking in lich water as we speak. And don't get me started on a gangland leader who—"

"Not going to work," she said.

"Then tell me what will work, K," I said, saying her name softly but forcefully.

K stepped forward. Her green eyes shone with determination. "You are the Lester Broussard I've heard so much about," she said. She rubbed her back. "You left a bruise when you threw that food tray. Anyway, I understand where you're coming from and that you don't want to see anyone get hurt. But I've made up my mind. There's nothing anyone can do—"

"To change it," I said sadly, finishing her sentence. "If I had a million dollars every time I heard that."

I looked around at the walls of shadow-spun lightning, the frozen timescape she had created with her shadowcraft. "So, what now? Since you're not going to listen, we might as well get this over with."

I gave a hand signal to Bo. The dead man pulled out a pistol and aimed it at her.

"I was hoping we wouldn't have to go the death-by-firing squad route," I said, seriously hoping she wasn't going to go down this path. But she was just Natkaal's puppet. A fate worse than death awaited her if she truly trusted the grasshopper.

The woman's jaw dropped upon seeing two guns pointed at her.

"That's not fair," she said with a smirk.

The next thing I knew, Bo and Harris were frozen on either side of me. K started walking toward me, staring at me with the utmost conviction as her smirk widened. The two of us stood in a narrow corridor surrounded by lightning-veined shadows.

Damn it. She closed the wall of shadows in on me. Now it was just me and her.

I pushed out a hand to both sides of the shadow corridor. The wall had nearly closed up to my shoulders.

"Let's try this again," she said. "Give me the suncatcher."

"Since you're going to try again, why don't I try again: hear what I'm saying, K. This path goes nowhere."

"Wrong answer," she said.

"Right back at you."

She was only a few feet away from me now, close enough to reach out and touch.

K gave a nervous look at the wall. Her face betrayed her for just a millisecond, but it was all I needed. She was losing control of her shadowcraft. Closing in the wall had taken more energy than she expected. If I was right, she wouldn't be able to hold up the wall much longer.

I reached into my winter coat and pulled out the crumpled paper bag. "You want it? Here it is."

I tossed it to her. She screamed in midair. "What the hell are you doing?" she cried as she caught the bag.

She unrolled the paper bag, reached in, and ripped out a perfect circle of stained glass. She jammed it into the sky and cried, "Here it is, Master!"

Except she had one problem. She was so desperate to get a

hold of the suncatcher that she didn't realize it wasn't the one she was looking for.

When nothing happened, her eyes moved up to the picture of Hazel between her fingers.

"No," she said, retreating. She bumped against the wall of shadow and almost dropped the suncatcher. "What have you done?"

I pulled out the evidence bag from my winter coat and produced the *real,* intact suncatcher. I held it up and said, "If you can't handle this, what makes you think you can handle Natkaal?"

K mouthed something, but I didn't hear it. The suncatcher shook in my hands and heated up. Suddenly, it was like warm asphalt in my hands. I looked up at it, but all I saw was blinding yellow light. Every bone in my body rattled. Strange grunting sounds escaped from my mouth like I was being jolted around by the worst wooden roller coaster in the world. Something enveloped me from below the ground, cemented my feet in place. Something far, far below grabbed my ankles, like a hot hand reaching out from the mantle of the earth. But the hand wasn't… a hand. It was pure, radiant energy that shot up through my body and out of my head. I opened my mouth to scream, or maybe I didn't. I didn't know what was real.

My arm locked into a 90-degree angle pointed at the sky. The light exploded through the suncatcher and broke away in 100 directions as if the suncatcher were a prism.

A noise shook me to my core and cooled my blood into ice water. The sound shook every nook and cranny in my body, making me at once regretful of this journey and at the same time confirming everything I knew to be true.

The sound, after it had shaken me a few hundred times, was a horse whinny laugh.

It was Natkaal. I was one with him, and he with me.

The grasshopper's wings spread and flapped like wind

turbines as the light faded. K dropped to her knees and put her suncatcher hand over her heart.

"Master! I exist to serve you," she said, staring at the ground.

And there I was, locked into place, forming what must have been Natkaal's thorax as he laughed again.

"I told you to stay out of this, Lester," Natkaal said. "This would normally be the part where I have my faithful servant end your life, but I will have to settle for the next best thing."

Natkaal's human hand—a golden torch of light—pointed at Harris, who was frozen with his gun pointed at where K had been a minute ago. "End this meddlesome detective."

K raised her head and produced a knife from her jacket. "My pleasure, Master."

CHAPTER SEVENTEEN

HARRIS WAS ABOUT TO DIE, and he wouldn't even know what hit him.

I was locked in place. I couldn't move even if I wanted to.

K raised the blade and prepared to launch it at Harris.

"Destroy the shadowcraft spell and plunge your blade into his heart just as time resumes," Natkaal said. "It will be quick and painless."

Suddenly, the suncatcher in K's other hand rattled. Hazel's tongue glowed as if animated, and the sunrise behind her blazed violently.

K stopped and stared at the suncatcher.

"Stop hesitating!" Natkaal shouted.

K dropped the suncatcher, but it wouldn't leave her hand. Rather, it stuck to her hand.

She cried out in pain as a beam of rainbow light erupted from the stained glass.

"No!" Natkaal cried. "You stupid amateur!"

The rainbow-colored light slammed into me, but I didn't feel it. Natkaal did, because the grasshopper let out a startled cry that ripped across the parking lot and through the wall of sound as if it were construction paper.

An explosion turned my vision orange. Then I was flying. Through the air. In a long, slow-motion arc. Asphalt swam up to meet me as I hit the ground.

K was in the air too, but she wasn't flying. Natkaal had her in one of his human hands. The grasshopper cursed her out and called her worthless before suplexing her to the ground.

All was quiet for a few seconds. An eternity passed in those seconds—me, on the ground, K on the ground, Natkaal gnashing his triangular teeth.

"This isn't over!" Natkaal cried as the light around him dissipated, then flashed like a supernova.

I woke to blinding sunlight and a bone-cold breeze.

"Boss man, boss man…"

Bo's bald head circled mine, circled the sun. A corona glinted off his left ear.

Two strong hands pulled me up and I sat on the grass, rubbing my head as the police station parking lot and the giant sycamore sharpened into view.

"That was a hard fall," Bo said, patting me on the back. "Take it easy."

"How long was I out?" I asked.

"Not that long," Bo said. "I think you'll live."

Bo held up the intact suncatcher, dangling it by its metallic chain. The grasshopper caught the light and twinkled in the breeze.

"Maybe don't use Natkaal's suncatcher next time," Bo said.

"You got that right," I said. "I did it for science. At least I know why that thing is so important now."

I heard Harris's voice. He was calling for an ambulance.

I swept my gaze across the parking lot until I spotted

Harris next to the picnic table. He was crouched over K's body, speaking into his phone.

My heart leaped into my throat when I saw her spreadeagled on the snow.

Bo said something to me, but I passed out again.

I woke to the sound of two women speaking in hushed tones.

First, my eyes didn't open. I heard them speaking against the faded grays of my mind's eye. I might as well have been floating.

My body was warm and cozy, like I was wrapped in a thick comforter. I wanted to go back to sleep. I wanted to stay here forever.

My eyes opened slowly as if of their own accord. My lids were as heavy as anvils. A gallery of bokeh lights swam around me. Two linear fluorescents were dimmed down low in the ceiling. A steady beeping tapped a cadence into the air.

Was it…a heart rate monitor?

I turned my head and the bokeh lights crab-danced around me until I settled onto human shapes that could have been close, but they might as well have been light-years away. One was dressed in white, the other beige. They were the two women. I only heard some of their words.

"No idea…he's been through," the woman in white said.

"He'll…all right. And he'll…just fine," the woman in beige said.

My eyelids were suddenly too heavy. They clanged shut and ushered in darkness and more of that sweet, sweet warmth.

My eyes opened again. This time, a black woman's face floated in front of mine. Dreads. Ruby earrings. A beautiful, unending smile.

A hand on my palm.

"So glad…back again," the woman said. Though she was near me, her voice was a distant dream. She might as well have been underwater. The lights dazzled in blurry balls behind her, and in my twilight, my lids began to shut again. But when the woman spoke, my lids stopped their rapid descent and I saw her through two narrow, fluttering slats.

Her warm hand patted mine.

"Is…anything…do for…?"

"Huh?" I asked.

The hand patted me again. "…there we can…you?"

My lips contorted into a goofy smile. I said something to her about wanting another bowl of Tabasco chicken noodle soup.

The woman didn't say anything at first. She didn't need to. Her warmth suffused through my hands, up my arms, and into my heart. My heartbeat slowed, and I felt my heart growing in my chest as warmth radiated out to my entire body.

I didn't need to see her. I didn't need to hear her. I could feel her. I've heard it said that 90 percent of human communication is nonverbal, and boy, did I understand that now.

The woman smiled again, opened her mouth and threw her head back into loud, joyful belly laughter. The kind of laugh that reminds you of a child. The kind of laugh not underpinned with any cares, weights of the world, or stress. Just—pure, blissful laughter.

And so clear—like someone reached into my brain, dialed the radio to a better frequency so I could hear all the highs, mids, and lows of her serene laugh and the beeping from the heart monitor and the murmur of the hospital doctors and nurses in the hallway and the birds outside chattering in the day.

I found myself laughing with her weakly. Then my eyelids clanged shut again and I drifted off into zenful sleep as she held my hand.

I woke up on a hospital bed to a steady metronome of beeping. My eyes focused, I took in a deep breath, and I looked side to side.

Of course, Bo was in a stiff-backed chair, reading a shiny tabloid. Though the lights were dimmed, he still wore his sunglasses. His loud tracksuit definitely jolted me to my senses; if I wasn't awake before, I was after seeing the ketchup and mustard.

"Welcome back, boss man," he said, folding the magazine on his lap.

I felt of myself, expecting an IV or broken bones. I was still in my winter coat. From my visit to the hospital earlier, I immediately knew that I was in the emergency room.

The air was clearer now. I could see. Hear every word Bo said. Somehow, I knew I was back to my senses.

I sighed. I wanted to see the woman again. I wanted to feel her warmth. I wanted to laugh.

I tried to laugh again. A weak belly laugh escaped my mouth, but it didn't have the same resonance.

I sat up, making myself laugh harder, but it ended with a cough and I had to stop myself from choking.

Bo rushed up and slapped me on the back. He hit me so hard, it was going to leave a mark.

"Didn't know laughing was a side effect of getting your lights knocked out."

"Not a side effect," I said, catching my breath. A tingling sadness spread across my body as I realized that the woman was indeed gone and that no amount of laughing I could do would bring me closer to her. Suddenly, I felt cold.

Bo slipped a hospital blanket over me.

"How long was I—" I asked, shivering.

"About an hour," Bo said, finishing my sentence. "But

that's not what you really want to know," he said, pursing his lips. "What you really want to know is who is next door."

I stared at him, catching some air. "Okay, tell me—who's next door?"

"Our girl."

I said the words a few times before I understood.

I cursed and threw the blanket to the floor. Bo stopped me from getting off the bed.

"Whoa whoa whoa. Take it easy."

"Sheeeeet," I said.

"Harris is with her. Trust me, boss man—she ain't going nowhere."

I settled in the bed, and Bo pushed a button on the side that angled my legs upward as the subtle white noise of a talk show filled the room among the beeping and quiet murmurs of doctors and nurses outside.

Bo put the blanket back on me and asked me if I wanted him to sing a lullaby. I swatted him away like a senile old man.

"Everything's under control," Bo said. "You'll see."

I settled down as my sudden wildness dissipated. "I guess I could rest for a minute."

"A minute?" Bo asked. "You need more than that, boss man."

I didn't think I'd be back at this hospital so soon. I had already been here one time too many.

A nurse walked in, asked me what I had been doing that led to my injuries. I pulled a page out of Harris's book and told her I had no idea. Her tone immediately shifted to what could best be described as cranky as she took my vitals, read me my rights, and told me that whatever I had been doing, I was lucky to be alive. I thanked her kindly, told her she could send the doctor's choice of pain meds to my pharmacy down the road from my house, and asked her when I could get the hell out of here, thank you very much.

As she told me the doctor would need to see me before

releasing me, Harris leaned in the doorway, arms folded. When she left, the boyish detective grinned at me and said, "You're learning fast. Good thing you don't have a criminal record."

"Or drugs in my system," I said. "Harris, what's the deal?"

Harris pulled the curtain to my room shut and pulled up a chair. He brought me and Bo in close and spoke quietly.

"Everyone's favorite grasshopper got away, but our amateur necromancer didn't. She's one bed over, and she's banged up just about as bad as I was when we had that fight at the pancake house. She's even got matching bruises and a busted lip."

I grimaced.

"That's not all," Harris said. He brought Bo and me in close and whispered, “We got her personal information. The woman formerly known as “K” is named Kay—K-A-Y—O'Malley. She's 41 years old, born and raised in the Lou, and she lives in North County. I told her we could do this the easy way or the hard way, and she chose the easy way."

The boyish detective flashed another grin. "Of course, she woke up handcuffed to the bed, but those are minor details."

Harris patted my foot. "Glad you're okay."

"You got lucky again," I said, swinging my legs off the bed and planting my feet on firm, cold floor. "She was going to kill you."

"Bo and I figured as much when one minute we were staring at her and the next, all hell had broken loose.”

"She awake?" I asked. "I want to speak with her."

Harris helped me out of bed and gestured me through the curtain and into the next room where Kay lay handcuffed to a hospital bed. Harris wasn't kidding about the busted lip. It was swollen to twice its size.

“Hey,” she said weakly. “Cold?”

I still had the hospital blanket wrapped around me, but I didn’t care. I ignored her joke.

I pulled up a chair. Bo and Harris stood like sentinels in the doorway.

"So I guess you were right after all," she said. She gave me a sad, steely look, then focused on the wall ahead.

"This sort of thing gives me no pleasure," I said.

"After all I did for him, he discarded me like trash."

"That's how it usually happens, Kay, but I won't stoop to telling you I told you so. How about you tell us what's been going on instead."

"Natkaal told me he could save him," Kay said.

Finally. Progress.

"Save who?"

Then it dawned on me. I pulled out the photograph Kay had dropped at the pancake house. I pointed to her husband.

She nodded. I went with my intuition—I decided to make assumptions and Kay would confirm or deny them. But I knew my assumptions weren't going to be wrong. Her story was my story.

"What kind of cancer did your husband have?" I asked point blank.

"Pancreatic."

I felt her pain. This was an intractable, incurable cancer that was better described as a death sentence. I thought back to my wife Amira's diagnosis, in the oncology office with the baby blue walls with the plush chairs and skeleton standing watch in the corner as a pudgy doctor told us that Amira had uterine cancer. Amira's hand had mine in a volcano-hot death-grip. I don't remember the words the doctor said. Everything was a blur…time stopped.

"—and we must begin an aggressive treatment immediately, Mrs. Broussard."

"Whatever we must do," Amira had said. She had such resolve in her voice.

I smelled her patchouli perfume again, as if she were here with me. There were only two hands in the world that felt like Amira's, and for a split second, I could feel her again.

"Lester?" Amira asked.

I stared at the baby blue walls, then at the grinning skeleton. Was it real? It couldn't have been real. And then I thought of the love of my life as a skeleton. My knees were weak.

"Lester?"

"Yes, right. Okay, doc."

Goddamn it, why did this have to happen to me? I wanted to cry. Despite Amira being the one with the diagnosis, I was the one who needed to be held.

"—a regimen of chemotherapy. It has risks. I'd like to talk through that with you, but—"

"Lester? Lester."

"I'm fine, baby."

"Can we have a moment?" Amira asked the doctor.

And then Amira's voice mixed with Kay's.

"He had stage IV," Kay said sadly. "They didn't catch it in time."

I cursed. I don't know what I would have done if it had been terminal. At least Amira and I had a fighting chance.

I blinked hard and pushed the memory out of my mind. I hadn't expected it to come upon me so suddenly.

Kay hadn't noticed. "The doctors gave him six months to live." She swallowed hard. "How was I supposed to live with half a heart, Lester?" she said, giving me an appraising, sorrowful look.

"I understand," I said.

"We went through the treatments. I kept telling myself there had to be more to life than this. The whole thing was so unfair. I thought we would grow old together and welcome grandchildren with loving arms."

"That's perfectly normal, Kay," I said.

"I fell asleep one night and I made a promise to anyone

who would listen. I said that if I could spend just one more year with Johnny, then I would do whatever it took. I didn't care what happened to me or my soul."

The indomitable will of the necromancer: Kay had it in spades. I remembered the seven stages of grief. In the bargaining stage, you're willing to make any outlandish deal you can. It doesn't make sense. It doesn't have to. If somebody told you that you had to transform into a bowl of Jell-O for a year but that you could see your loved one again for just one minute, you'd gladly turn into a pile of jiggling lime gelatin on the spot.

Kay continued, "As I fell asleep one night, someone spoke to me. At first, I thought it was a lucid dream. Why wouldn't it be? No one ever speaks back during those long, dark nights of the soul. It told me that it understood my predicament. Offered me condolences. It told me that this was not a hallucination and that I was very much awake. It told me not to open my eyes, but to focus on my mind's eye. It told me to think about Johnny. It told me that Johnny was going to die, but that fate wasn't written in ink. It could be changed."

"Let me guess: it was the grasshopper."

She shook her head. "I didn't know who it was at the time. But I couldn't resist the offer. It told me exactly what to do. Johnny didn't believe me at first, but then he heard the voice too. We had nothing to lose, so we obeyed."

I leaned in, riveted.

"We planned every little detail. Johnny was to rent an apartment a few blocks away under a fake name. We spent weeks learning about the dark art. Natkaal told us everything, and we were ready. At the next waning crescent moon, he gave us the signal."

"Kay," I said quietly, knowing what was coming next.

"Natkaal killed Johnny, didn't he?" I asked. An uncomfortable knot formed in my stomach. "The logic was that he was going to die anyway, right?"

Kay pursed her lips. The gesture caused her pain. She didn't have to say any more.

"It was part of the plan so I could see Johnny again in a new form," Kay said. "And that damned grasshopper lied to me. I was supposed to reunite with Johnny, but the grasshopper made up some excuse about the lich lakes being closed and not being able to see him. He said there was a major obstacle."

She glanced at Harris. The boyish detective went pale.

Natkaal had fed her a convenient lie. Of course Harris had nothing to do with the real problem of the lakes being closed—Halgeron's absence. After Kay killed Harris, the grasshopper would have given her another excuse.

"Now I realize how foolish I was," Kay said. She stared at me, her eyes full of terror. "Lester, what have I done?"

"A lot, but there'll be time to talk about that later," I said. "What about the suncatcher?"

"It's a work of lightcraft," Kay said. "Natkaal taught me how to create it and channel light energy. He told me it is the strongest magic. He told me that it can only be summoned from the middle of a shadowcraft spell. It's a magic so rare and unique that it requires an unbelievable cost."

"What's the cost?"

"The length of time one must submit to liches."

I paused. Shadowcrafting took minutes off your life in proportion to the duration of the spell. If what Kay was saying was right, lightcraft *increased* the amount of time you spent in the presence of liches. That begged the question of where one went after leaving a lich's custody.

I've heard of souls marinating in lich lakes for hundreds if not thousands of years, and it didn't have anything to do with morality. It had to do with self-reflection. Some people had a lot more self-reflection to do than others. I'm fairly certain that a necromancer would have a lot more spiritual thinking to do than your neighbor next door. But no one knew for sure. I didn't know why it never dawned on me to ask CeCe about this. Part of me didn't want to know.

"How do you use lightcraft?" I asked.

"You focus your thoughts," she said. "You need an object that channels the light. A suncatcher was the perfect artifact. In the center of the shadowcraft spell, you simply imagine what you need, and it bubbles up from below."

"Below," I repeated. "From the spirit world?"

That explained why Natkaal had appeared in shimmering light. Lightcraft was a way to communicate.

My brain hurt as I tried to understand the grasshopper's motive. He was still several leaps ahead of me.

"I can help you," Kay said. "I know both crafts. You don't."

"True, but you have one problem." I tapped the rails of her hospital bed. "You're under doctor's orders."

"And under arrest," Harris said.

Kay regarded my words then struggled against the handcuff. "Like it or not, I'm your only hope."

Bo chuckled. "You offer assistance by telephone?"

Kay settled back into her hospital bed.

"With your injuries, you'd be a liability to yourself," I said. "It sounds like you're going to be here for a few days anyway. We'll be back. Besides, I should have enough to take it from here."

We left her on the hospital bed, staring at the wall.

CHAPTER EIGHTEEN

There we were, back in my garage, back to the place where the Hazel suncatcher was born. I had an idea and I needed to verify whether it would work.

I switched on the overhead fluorescent bulbs and they buzzed awake, dimming a few times before they bloomed to full brightness. I hadn't cleaned up from my prior session; my sawhorse stood in the middle of the floor and leftover stained glass twinkled on it as if trying to get my attention.

"Nice tools," Harris said, brushing the back of one of my drills with a knuckle. He gave my wall of pegboards an approving nod.

"You need anything built, boss man's your man," Bo said. "Sometimes I think Lester can fix anything."

"I never was handy," Harris said. He ran a hand through a bin full of screws, jangling them around. "My old man was. Always gave me hell about not being able to use tools."

"Tools aren't as intimidating as they seem," I said, gathering the stained-glass shards into my hand and letting them rustle into a plastic bag. "The first half of the battle is knowing what tool you need. The second is learning how to use it. Then, you file that information in the back of your head until it comes out one day unannounced, and you look like a hero."

I grabbed my glass cutter and held it up for Harris. The cylindrical shaft was as heavy as a river rock. "I haven't used a glass cutter since I was eighteen. You'd think after all these years that I'd have forgotten how to use it, but the muscle memory remains. Like riding a bicycle."

"Easier said than done," Harris said. "You ought to see me with a hammer sometime."

"So you're one of those put-your-entire-life-on-pegboards kind of guys, huh?" Harris asked, studying my collection of rulers and protractors.

"I take offense to that," I said playfully.

I never thought I'd be in my garage so much with the dark art. But I couldn't stop thinking about what Kay had told me. For the first time in a long time, I was starting to put the pieces together.

Shadowcraft. Magic strong enough to stop time that sapped the caster's life energy. Lightcraft. A magic so bright and mysterious that it could channel up the spirit world.

Natkaal, whose aspirations were to be an archdemon. A series of suncatchers that caught the light and allowed him to push into this world like a hand pushing through a bed of iron filings.

"Do you have the answers to those questions I asked you?" I asked Harris.

Harris slid out a notebook from his pocket and tapped it. "Why did you want to know about Kay's husband?" he asked.

I had asked him to look up everything he could about Kay's husband, just to crosscheck what she told me. I wasn't 100 percent positive she was on our side. Like any good criminal, she changed her tune the moment she landed in handcuffs.

"Kay's husband's name was Johnny O'Malley," Harris said, tapping his notebook with a pencil.

"Were you able to verify the identity of the body?" I asked.

"We're working on it. I should have an official confirmation in the next day or so, but I'm pretty sure the John Doe in the apartment is him."

I folded my arms. Though I agreed with Harris, there was something else I couldn't shake. Something else just outside of my understanding.

"Kay said Johnny was diagnosed with cancer. Can we also verify that?"

"Also working on it," Harris said with a winsome smile. He tucked his notebook into his pocket and his pencil behind his ear. "We're at an impasse."

"For the moment," I said, frowning. "But that's why we're here, Detective."

Bo tapped his temple and wagged a finger at me. "Ha, I see what you're doing, boss man."

I paused and turned to him. "Enlighten me."

"You don't trust Kay," Bo said, "and you got no way of verifying anything she told you. You also don't think she's lying, but see, you're hedging your bets."

"I'm following you, big man," Harris said. "I like where you're going this time."

With lightning rapidity, Bo grabbed a nail from a bin and chucked it at Harris. Harris ducked just in time. The nail bounced off the wall and dribbled across the floor.

"What do you mean *this time*?" Bo asked playfully. "You know I'm always the one who comes up with ideas to save the day."

"Okay then, Mr. Saves the Day," I said. "How are you going to save the world this time?"

"Ain't no thang, really," Bo said, as if the answer was the simplest thing in the world. "Check it out: all you gotta do is cut your palm, take a quick visit to the other side, and verify the information over there," he said. "Like I said before, ain't no thang but a chicken wang."

Bo had a point.

I wasn't quite there yet though. I wanted to take things a little slower. I was playing multidimensional chess with a demon, after all.

"Not bad," I told Bo, "but you just described step two."

"Step two?" Bo and Harris said at the same time.

I held up the suncatcher and grinned. "I need to pay a visit to the dark side."

CHAPTER NINETEEN

Our destination was only a few minutes away. Bo didn't like my idea one bit, and I didn't blame him. I was taking a gamble, one that would literally shave time off my life.

I was visiting a witch adept in shadowcraft.

Camille Steverson was originally my enemy during my last adventure. She became a friend at the last minute, helping me lift Natkaal's soul curse and save the city from a vitriolic feud between the grasshopper demon and two aging witches who cast the curse on him. The elderly witches were over 200 years old, born during the slavery era. Natkaal had cursed them too, and the curse prevented them from dying. The Steverson sisters lived in aging agony, far longer than any human should have lived. Their bodies gave out on them, and they couldn't even communicate. It was their great-great-great-granddaughter, Camille, who became the architect of the master plan to lift Natkaal's soul curse.

Camille was a skilled witch trained by her grandmother, one of the sisters. When I lifted the soul curse, the Steverson sisters died, releasing Camille from a heavy caretaking burden. She was now free to live her life without the invisible chains that had bound her for so long.

I had called ahead to let her know I was coming. We kept in touch; her twin sister, Cassandra, had gotten engaged to a young man named Gillian. Bo and I sent them an engagement gift. Camille lived in a sprawling mansion in the city. She became the leader of her grandmother's coven. I didn't know how the Steverson sisters accumulated all that wealth to afford such a huge mansion. I didn't want to know.

Bo eased my Town Car out of my back alley. Bo ground his teeth as we rode in silence to the mansion. Harris listened with intrigue as I told him all about Camille and her skill with shadowcraft.

"Why would anyone want to cast spells like that?" Harris asked.

"Why would anyone want to speak to the dead?" I asked. "It's all about getting slight advantages. In the supernatural world, any advantage is power. Accumulate enough advantages and you become unstoppable."

"Unstoppable," Harris said, repeating after me. "She must be powerful."

"A little too powerful," Bo said. "She almost took me and boss man out."

“Using shadowcraft," I said. "If anyone can give us some tips on what Natkaal might be up to, it's Camille."

Bo said nothing as he slowed to a stop at a red light. I knew something wasn't right.

"Lay it on me," I said.

"You're going to pay a big price," Bo said. "This stuff ain't nothing to mess around with, man. It's not a good idea."

I nodded. "We have to stay one step ahead of Natkaal. Unless you can think of a better way—"

"We're talking time off your life," Bo said, turning to me. "Do you know how it's going to end for you?"

I regarded the question. It was intentionally rhetorical.

"Of course not," Bo said. "Almost nobody knows when they're going to die, boss man. What if you're spending time with Malcolm? Or you're in the middle of an adventure? And then—bam! —You're in the spirit world."

I crossed my arms. "I considered that," I said solemnly.

"And think about all the people you won't be able to help because of this decision right now."

I waved the comment away, but Bo was right. I didn't want to think about my bitter end and the pain it would cause those around me.

The red light shifted to green, and Bo passed smoothly through an intersection.

Harris reached up and leaned on the space between the driver and passenger front seats. The leather creaked as he put his weight on them. "If it makes you feel any better, Bo, you'll depart for the spirit world with Lester at the same time."

"This ain't about me," Bo said. "It's about Marlese and Malcolm."

"I hear you," I said, "but if I don't stop the grasshopper, no one will."

My phone buzzed in my breast pocket, cutting the tension and making me jump. Sure enough, it was my daughter.

The city buildings blurred by outside as I put the phone to my ear and focused on my baby girl.

"Hey, Mar."

"You're just going to leave me hanging, aren't you?" she asked. If the irritation in her voice were a knife, it would've cut my cheek.

"What's wrong?" I asked.

"I've been trying to get in touch with you about the tuxedo fitting," she said. "I've been calling you and calling you."

"Sorry," I said, lowering my phone for a moment and swiping over to my voicemails. She *had* been calling. I hadn't noticed because my phone was on silent. My stomach twinged with guilt.

"Well?" she asked. "I've been trying to call The Whispering Pines Tuxedo Company, but they are not picking up the phone either. Did they show up at your house?"

I groaned. I had forgotten to tell her.

"About that—"

"Oh no," Marlese said. "Please don't tell me he stood you up. I don't know how I'm going to find another company. You have no idea how much work it was to find them."

"He showed up, Mar," I said quickly. "He took our measurements just fine. He was a delightful guy."

Marlese went silent. I could hear her face contorting into skepticism. "But?"

I told her about what happened, about how the gangly man had fallen down my steps, injured himself, and died during surgery.

"Oh my God," she said.

"I'm beside myself about it," I said. "That's why I haven't called. I'm sorry."

"I just don't have any luck," Marlese said. Her voice was sad. I wish I could reach through the phone and hug her. This was definitely going to set her wedding back.

"Bo and I are occupied right now, but when we're free, we'll research some tuxedo shops here in St. Louis. Don't despair, sweetheart. We'll figure this out. Even if Bo has to endure some funny stares, he will manage."

"Yeah, I guess," she said. After a moment of silence, she said, "Are you going to the funeral?"

Funeral… I hadn't thought about that.

"I'd like to," I said, "but the cops are having a difficult time locating his family. I don't know if there will be one."

"Then you should at least pay your respects," she said. "I wouldn't want this hanging over my head."

"I'm working on it," I said.

I told her I loved her and to kiss my grandson for me. She hung up.

I had lost track of where we were. Now, we were

surrounded by enormous stone mansions and wrought-iron fences. Bo navigated down a serpentine residential street lined with hedges and tall, mature trees. We approached an enormous limestone mansion with topiary sculptures and a tall weeping willow in the front yard. Bo slowed down and engaged the turn signal, nosing the car up to a black gate with the letter S in the center.

"Holy crap," Harris said under his breath.

The mansion was the size of five large family homes. Its gray exterior was immaculate, and the hedges lining the first floor were flawlessly trimmed. A topiary of a candle stood proudly in the middle of a car circle, though the hedge was slightly brown due to the winter season. The gates clicked and whirred open, and Bo drove down the long road to the portico over the front door.

“Black magic money,” Bo said, shifting the car into park once we were under the shade of the portico. “It’ll be good to see Camille, though.”

“She might teach me a thing or two,” Harris said. “I could use it in my work.”

“Let’s not all go shaving minutes off our lives, now,” I said.

The walkway to the door was paved in smooth red bricks that ran up to the door in a symmetrical V pattern. The front door was a tall black double door with half-moon windows and golden handles. Two security cameras perched high above the door, angling and tracking us as we walked to the door.

“Just a moment,” a female voice said through an intercom that buzzed next to the door.

I dug my hands in my pockets and glanced around the mansion. Shades were drawn over the windows on the first floor.

“You can just smell the money,” I said, studying the golden handles on the door.

“What do you think it would be like to live in a place like

this?" Harris asked. "Reminds me of a horror novel I read once."

Bo and I turned to stare at him.

"Beautiful lady lives in a giant mansion all by herself," Harris said. "One rainy night, a crazy ax-murdering psychopath in a raccoon mask breaks in. The whole book is her running through the house to escape him."

"And?" Bo asked, raising an eyebrow. "Does she survive?"

"Ax to the neck," Harris said, making a cutting motion against his neck. "Last chapter. Then the killer takes his mask off and it turns out that it was actually the woman who lived in the house the whole time. Split personality or something."

"Sounds like the next great American novel," I said sarcastically.

"Anyway, must be tough living in this place all alone," Harris said.

"Who said she lived alone?" I asked.

Footsteps tracked toward the door. The black door swung open slowly.

Camille Steverson wore a Ramones t-shirt, ripped acid-washed jeans, and pearly white skateboard shoes. The last time I saw her, she had a bushy afro; today, it was styled into tight cornrows with braids that curled to an end on her shoulders. Her chestnut eyes were bright and lively, and her coffee-colored skin glowed like a model's. She seemed so much lighter than when I saw her last. I chalked it up to being free at last, but I didn't forget her power for one moment. Behind her sweet exterior was a cold, hard witch who wouldn't think twice about stopping time to kill you if it meant protecting her family. You'd be dead before you even realized what happened.

"It's not every day that I get a visit from a necromancer," she said, crossing the threshold.

"It's not every day a necromancer needs to visit a witch," I said. I kissed her on the cheek.

Camille shook Bo's hand.

I introduced Harris; after a quick exchange of howdy dos, Camille motioned for us to enter.

"I imagine we have a lot to discuss," she said, crossing back into the house. "Come on in. Make yourselves comfortable."

Harris entered first, looking up at a massive glass chandelier in the foyer of the lobby. Then Bo entered, slipping off his sunglasses as he studied the ornate marble floor. I entered last.

Rather, I tried to enter. The moment I crossed the threshold, a pentacle flashed in front of me, its tips blood red. A shockwave ripped through me.

The next thing I knew, I was flying through the air. My heart pounded as I slid to a stop in the grass three yards from the house.

"Sheeeeet…"

"Yo, boss man!" Bo cried. "You a'ight?"

I stared up at the blue sky as my brain caught up with what the hell just happened.

I sat up, tasting ash and cinder on my tongue. The air around me sparkled with golden dust. Residues from a ward.

Bo, Harris, and Camille came running. Bo pulled me to my feet and Harris brushed grass off me.

"Talk about seeing stars," I said, remembering the blood-red pentacle. The damn thing practically burned in my mind's eye as I thought about it.

"My wards have been going a little haywire lately," Camille said. "I'm so sorry. These are old-school wards my grandmother installed. They repel first and let me ask questions later. They're starting to show their wear and I need to replace them with something smoother and more modern."

I waved her comment away and caught my breath.

"But just to check," she said. "Anything you want to tell me about?"

"Not that I know of," I said, panting.

"You're not possessed by any demons, are you?"

"If I was, I wouldn't be here."

"You haven't been cursed?"

"Sometimes I think being a necromancer is a curse," I said, smirking. "But no."

"Hmm," Camille said. "Let's try again."

We passed my Town Car. Harris brushed more grass and dirt from my coat, and a giant clod sloughed off my waist and smacked onto the pavement next to the car.

I stood for a moment, reorienting myself before catching up to Camille, who stood with her arms folded.

"Ready to try again?" she asked.

I nodded. Camille watched, concerned, as I stepped across the threshold again. This time, I passed right through and into the insanely luxurious lobby.

She shrugged. "My fault. Let me make you a coffee as an apology."

I sighed with relief as we followed Camille deeper into the house.

CHAPTER TWENTY

Camille's kitchen was as big as my entire house. There was a culinary-grade range with six burners, a refrigerator the width of my Town Car, and a wine cooler with a pyramid of dark bottles in its depths. Immense French doors and angled clerestories drenched the kitchen in sunlight as Camille let us in and gestured for us to sit at a long granite island whose surface seemed to sparkle.

Bo glanced around the kitchen and nodded with approval, pointing out her appliances. He went ga-ga when he saw the label on her range—it was the kind they promoted all the time on cooking channels.

"God, the kind of food I could cook on this puppy," he said, running a hand along a cast-iron burner.

"It's not as good as you think," Camille said, working at a coffee machine next to a sink with an ornate bronze goose-neck faucet. A ruby red coffee maker ticked and breathed a final sigh of brew, ushering a wave of an exotic dark coffee blend across the kitchen. "I have to service it a few times a year, and it's expensive."

"Doesn't seem like that's a problem for you," I said.

Camille laughed. "Me and the coven do okay. Most of

them are traveling right now, so it's just me and a few others here in town. When the coven members make money on the various jobs they take, ten percent of it comes back to our trust fund. That takes care of the house, but the last year has been a little tight now that my grandmothers don't have us up to more…nefarious goals."

She winked at me. "There was nothing they wouldn't do to stop the grasshopper. It just so happened that with the darkness came a lot of money. I've committed to stopping that."

"Having the money to buy cooking equipment like that might make me reconsider being a good guy," Bo said, still staring at the range. "Damn."

"Don't sell out over an industrial range," Harris joked. "A good plate of beef brisket isn't worth selling your soul."

"I'll drink to that," I said.

"Mmm hmm," Bo said, pursing his lips and not taking his eyes off the range. "Eat the brisket first and then talk to me."

Camille served Harris and me white porcelain mugs with black coffee. The bitter coffee sobered me up from my dust-up with the house's ward.

Camille eased into a bar stool at the island, propped her head on her hands, and said, "What's up, gentlemen?"

"I'm helping my friend here with official police business," I said.

Camille's gaze shifted to Harris.

"Paranormal crimes, mmm?" she asked. "I had no idea such a department existed."

She sipped her coffee and gave Harris a smile. "The Steverson coven will not be a problem for you. Feel free to call on us when you need our expertise."

Harris brightened at the offer. "That would be great."

I told Camille everything—about Natkaal, the suncatcher, Kay, and the fight at the police station.

Camille listened intently. After I finished, it was a while

before she said anything. She stared outside, her eyes rapidly calculating what I just told her. Then she frowned.

"I'll gladly help you since the grasshopper's involved," she said. "And he's up to no good."

"Camille, what can you tell us about lightcraft?" I asked.

"It's a very powerful but very specific type of spell," she said. "I've never used it."

My heart sank.

"But my grandmother did once or twice," she said quickly. "You see, there are only three uses for lightcraft. The first is to communicate between worlds."

I remembered Natkaal pushing through into this world from the spirit world. It was clearly how he manipulated Kay.

"The second use is to find something," Camille said. "It can find anything that is lost, except there's a catch: in finding what you seek, you lose a part of yourself."

"Lose?" I asked.

"It's one of the sick jokes of the universe, like shadowcraft. With shadowcraft, you lose time from your life. With lightcraft, you lose time from your next life. When we pass from this world into the next, we undergo a supernatural therapy of sorts. The liches are the therapists."

"We marinate in lich water," I said, finishing her thought. "We atone for our sins, realize all of the great wrongs we've committed in our lives, and so on."

Camille shook her head. "It's more than that. It's a supernatural accounting of the soul. When the average person dies, their soul is intact. There is no person too messed up for liches to repair. But when you've used lightcraft, a piece of your soul becomes dislodged. That's not so easy for liches. It takes them longer to work on you, and therefore it takes *you* longer to achieve your true universal understanding. This creates more problems than you realize. First, it messes with the very fabric of fate itself. It also attracts the ire of angels."

Her comment took my breath away. "Angels?"

"Where do you think the light comes from?" Camille asked. "I may be a witch, but there are certain forces I don't mess with. Demons are one—you remember what happened to my grandmother, obviously. Angels are another."

I sat, stunned. I had heard of angels, but in my line of work, naturally, I never encountered any.

"So Natkaal is so hell-bent on becoming an archdemon that he would risk pissing off heavenly forces?"

"He won't piss them off," Camille said. "Whoever he's working with will draw the angels' anger. Remember, demons don't marinate in lich water. When they die, they *die*. But if he can get an unwitting human to cast the spell for him—"

"He gets the spell for free," Harris said, frowning. "Freaking cheapskate."

"And the necromancer breaks their soul apart without even realizing it," I said. "Kay is screwed."

I shook my head at the realization. Suddenly, the coffee didn't taste so good anymore.

"That's why lightcraft is rarely used," Camille said. "It can only be used in the middle of a shadowcraft spell. That's by design."

"How does one cast a shadowcraft spell so they can use lightcraft?" I asked.

Camille's eyes widened. "You're crazy, Lester."

"Sue me," I said. "How do you do it?"

I stared at her over the top of my glasses. "I'm not leaving until you tell me."

"It's your funeral," she said.

"You're damn right it is."

She sighed. "Fine. To cast a shadowcraft spell, you must have a connection to your target. When I cast a shadowcraft spell on you, it was because you were connected to Natkaal, and Natkaal was the bane of my grandmother. If you're wanting to use the spell on Natkaal, that's easier. It just requires a special intent; you must focus inward on the enmity you have for the target. You must want their destruction more than anything else in the world, but you must also have the restraint to think clearly and not give yourself to rage. Shadowcraft is right on the edge of insanity."

"Wonderful," I said.

"You asked for it," Camille said. "Once you've locked in your intent, you must visualize the field where you want time to stop. The bigger the field, the harder the spell, and the more you risk losing yourself. Then, just imagine time stopping. It takes about a minute for the spell to work."

"It's that simple?" I asked.

Camille laughed. "Of course it is. That's why the cost is so terrible, Lester. The only people who can cast the spell are those with enmities toward others. The magic is not designed for someone to use randomly. Since there must be a mental and spiritual connection between the caster and the target, most could not use it anyway. The cost scares away all but the most driven individuals—those who have nothing to lose."

Bo clucked his tongue and looked away. "That explains Kay and how she was able to target you, Lester. She was following Natkaal's orders and feeding on the grasshopper's enmity for you."

"And once I've activated the spell, then I hold up the suncatcher to activate a lightcraft spell, right?" I asked, showing her the suncatcher of Hazel. The witch took it in her hands and held it up to the light, nodding in approval before returning it to me.

"Lightcraft works by attracting light to a dark source. You need an interface for the light—a suncatcher is perfect for that. Once the light connects with you, you can perform your intended action. But be careful. You don't have long. Lightcraft spells are notoriously brief."

She rose. "That's all I know."

I downed the remainder of the coffee and grimaced as the strong blend went down. "I'll owe you a favor for this."

"And don't you forget it," she said, walking us out.

Camille stood with arms folded at her front door as we walked back to my Town Car. A gentle breeze blew in my face as I reached the car.

I stopped and turned to Camille.

"You said there were three uses for lightcraft," I said, remembering the conversation. "Communication, search, and?"

Camille's forehead wrinkled as she recalled her magical knowledge. "Banishing dark forces."

"You're kidding."

"Lightcraft exists to split the darkness," Camille said. "It's the spell's original purpose."

"Ah," I said, thinking.

A speck of brown drew my eye to the pavement. It was the dirt clod that Harris had brushed off my coat. But it was more than dirt.

I bent down and inspected it. Among the specks of dirt were curled legs like angle brackets raised to the sky. They were attached to a thick chocolate-colored shell. I scrunched my face up as I scrutinized the dead cockroach.

I looked back and forth between the roach and Camille's front door a few times, imagining the pentacle in the threshold that had flashed just before it launched me across the yard.

A cockroach. A *dead* cockroach.

A mansion like this didn't have cockroaches. Roaches like this didn't live outside. They—

I patted my coat immediately like it was on fire. I tore it off and shook it, then slapped it furiously on the ground. I invented a few curse words that would have made Bo clap in any other circumstance.

"What is it, boss man?" Bo asked. It took him a few seconds to spot the roach.

"Damn it!" I growled.

"What is it?" Harris asked. "Yikes. Is that another roach?"

I cursed. Again. And again. I chastised myself for being so stupid; then my heart stopped at the thought of Hazel and my spiders at home alone. My stomach churned. I wanted to vomit.

I barked at Bo and Harris to get in the car.

"Yo, chill, boss man," Bo said.

"It's the cockroaches," I said.

"I hate 'em too," Bo said.

"No, it's the cockroaches!" I said again. "All this time. We haven't had a cockroach problem."

Bo looked at me, confused.

"Bo," I said sharply. "We have a demon problem."

CHAPTER TWENTY-ONE

A RASH of gray clouds gathered in the sky as Bo tore down the streets of my neighborhood.

The grasshopper had fooled me again.

In the backseat, Harris stared outside resolutely, ready for a fight. Bo drove tight-jawed. I seethed with rage.

This was my fault.

I hadn't put two and two together that the cockroaches in my home were demons. Hadn't I fought enough of the buggers to know that they came in all forms?

Bo sped through a red light and a muscle car honked at him as I recalled how the grasshopper had fooled me.

I had wizard-grade wards installed in my home. I did this because Natkaal recommended them as a safety tactic against Camille and her coven, who nearly punched my ticket out of this world in my backyard. Natkaal called in a favor from a local wizard who installed said wards while Bo and I investigated the coven. I was poisoned with aconite at the time, and I wasn't in my right mind.

I knew Hank Garbo; he could be a certified asshole, but a deceiver he was not. That led me back to Natkaal. I heard his horse whinny laugh as I remembered that he watched disinterestedly as the wizard installed the wards. No spell was ever perfect; if there were any weaknesses, the grasshopper knew them. He would have watched as Garbo installed every ward, noting every weakness…and every mistake. He wouldn't have acted on the knowledge with his soul curse intact, but with the curse lifted, the information was now valuable to him. It made me question if this wasn't the plan all along.

I cursed again as Bo careened around a corner. A homeless man with a shopping cart at a crosswalk jumped out of our way and cursed us out in the rearview mirror.

We were three blocks away from home.

I balled my fists so hard that my fingernails dug into my palms. I wanted to summon up the strongest hellfire from the depths and roast the grasshopper and whatever minion was in my home.

Two blocks.

I couldn't take this cat-and-mouse game anymore. Something was going to give. I was the one who had the least to lose. I was about to prove it.

One block.

The tires screeched as Bo wrenched the steering wheel. The car lurched to one side. I leaned into the curve as gravel flew up around us. My Town Car whistled through the alley like an arrow before Bo slid to a stop in front of my garage.

I opened the glove box and handed our trusty pistol to Bo, told him to pocket it.

"Both of you listen very carefully," I said.

Bo and Harris watched me intently.

"When we get out of the car, it's going to be business as usual. We're going to walk up through the backyard quietly. Don't say *anything*. I want both of you to wait in the backyard. Don't stand in front of the door. Each of you take a side of the yard. Stay as close to the fence as possible."

"You need backup in there," Harris said, his eyes defiant.

"I'll need backup *outside*," I said. "Trust me."

"And if this plan fails?" Harris asked.

"I'll die," I said flatly, "and so will Natkaal. Then you won't have a problem anymore."

"Touché," the boyish detective said with a slow, sad smile. "But don't die on us, man."

Like a cavalry riding to war, we got out of the car and executed the plan.

It took everything for me to not run to the house as we stalked through my backyard over snow and dead weeds. I wanted to break through the back door. I couldn't. Hazel's safety was depending on me.

As we neared the house, I heard her barking. It was a stressed, aggressive bark. The three of us looked at each other nervously.

My heart stopped for a moment. *Get it together, Lester*, I said under my breath. *The fight will be here in a minute. Then you can give 'em hell.*

I crept up the steps to the back porch. Harris and Bo fanned out to the flanks of the backyard.

I opened the screen door and slid my key into the lock. I stopped for a moment and listened. Hazel's bark came from the kitchen. She hadn't noticed us approaching.

I grabbed the doorknob and remembered Camille's advice.

I focused, dredging up the waves of enmity deep within me—fury at Natkaal and whatever minion that was living surreptitiously in my home. I held Natkaal's insect face in my mind's eye, imagined him laughing that horse whinny laugh, then gnashing his teeth, then turning up his insect face at the very notion that I would be upset at him doing what demons did best—deceiving.

All of the hurt, pain, anger, and frustration welled up in my breast like the waves of an ocean just before a storm. I let the waves swell and swell and swell until they took over me.

The only thing I wanted was justice. Cold, righteous justice. I wouldn't be denied.

For a split second, I knew these emotions within me to be darkness. I felt only a small pang of regret, that I shouldn't have been giving myself to these feelings. But the furious waves washed over me again like the ocean swallowing a lone sailor after a shipwreck. The current dragged those feelings of righteousness all the way down to the damned bottom of my soul, never to be heard of again. At least for now.

Above, the clouds blistered in the sky as if responding to my feelings. The basso rumble of thunder underscored the air. Lightning struck nearby in the corner of my eye.

A thunderstorm in winter.

No, the shadowcraft spell. It was taking hold. The clock was counting down now until the spell reached critical mass and stopped time. Sixty seconds was all I had.

I inhaled as a lightning-veined wall of billowing shadows closed in around the house, suffocating the air. Before, this had been the telltale signs of a trap. Now it was my advantage.

I became aware of the metal doorknob in my hand. Every breath took twice as long. My heart thumped in my chest. Time slowed to a crawl.

I opened the door and slipped inside. The lights on my porch were turned off. Hazel's barking was slightly louder now. Every hair on the back of my neck stood up.

Bark, bark, growl. Growl…Bark. Bark.

I didn't know doggy Morse code, but I knew enough about my sweet pea to know that something was bothering her.

I was in the presence of something. Something big. Something dark and demonic. It made my stomach drop.

I crouched, moving across my shadowed porch, and passed a haphazard mess of shoe racks on the floor that I had never gotten around to organizing. I put a hand on the kitchen door, put my ear to the wood. Hazel was there. I moved swiftly and silently into the kitchen.

Hazel was facing me, barking at the radiator in the kitchen. She was barking at…nothing?

No—something was on the wall just above the radiator. A brown speck. A distressed cockroach raced back and forth across the wall.

I stood next to Hazel.

"Stand down, sweet pea."

Hazel did not stand down. Her attack stance was as ferocious as her bark.

I lost track in my mind how much time had passed. I didn't have much left. Every second counted now.

I pointed at the brown cockroach, and said, "I know who you are. Come out and show yourself."

Home is a sacred place. It doesn't matter the type—only beings who are meant to dwell in a home are allowed there. Nothing can remain concealed when the owner knows its presence. That's why they call home "home sweet home." It's just about the only place you can be safe in the supernatural world. If you couldn't be safe at home, you couldn't be safe anywhere. It was time to rid my home of this unwanted invader so I could make my home a home again and get my privacy back.

"I command you to show yourself," I said sharply.

The roach froze on the wall. Suddenly, two more roaches crawled up from behind the radiator.

And then there were three. Ten. Twelve. Fifteen. Damn it, I lost count.

I called Hazel's name, told her to retreat, but she kept barking and growling. I wished that I had my gun, but time was still on my side. Time *had* to be on my side.

The radiator overflowed with giant German cockroaches now. The entire thing was a living, breathing mass of clicking, hissing cockroaches. Their wings beat against their shells, fluttering like a mad flock of birds. The roaches assimilated into each other, their shells melting and reforming into a solid mahogany mass. A sour smell wafted into the air, like months-old rancid butter and curdling cheese. I scrunched my nose immediately.

The kitchen filled briefly with smoke. When it cleared, an enormous German cockroach stood in front of me. It stood on its rearmost hindlegs. One of its topmost legs carried a jagged rusted sword that looked of Arabic origin. A pair of fuzzy antennae waved wildly atop the roach's head. Two coal-black gridded eyes stared at me murderously, and under them, a tongue as long as a cobra swung back and forth, dripping hot saliva on my hardwood floor. The roach hunched over and let out a deep male, hoarse, stentorian laugh. The laugh rattled my bones.

In a flash, time stopped.

Hazel froze in mid-bark. The roach demon's mouth of serrated triangular teeth was open in a contorted curse that clearly meant me harm.

The shadowcraft spell had finally activated and reached critical mass. I sighed with relief.

I thrust my hand into my coat's interior pocket and brought out the suncatcher of Hazel. The glass gleamed in my hand. I pointed it at the roach and shouted, "Get the hell out of my house!"

An explosion tore across the room, followed by a rush of cold. I flew through the air.

I landed on my back. I was in the middle of my paved brickway that cut through my backyard. I held up my hands in front of my face as timbers and shards of glass fell all around me.

Hazel lay in the grass near me.

It was so bright, I couldn't see a damn thing. Yet I trusted the lightcraft to do its job just like Camille told me it would. A hard thud confirmed my belief. Then the lightcraft and shadowcraft faded into the wintry day.

The blast had blown a roach demon-sized hole in my

kitchen wall and back porch. I could see the kitchen. I wasn't happy about that. I also wasn't happy to have an unwanted spy in my home.

Nearby, on opposite ends of the yard, Bo and Harris were frozen, staring at the house with concern. They had no idea what was coming yet.

I jumped up and swiped a shovel off the ground. I held it like a baseball bat as I crept toward the roach demon lying on its back in my grass. The blast had hit it, but its body hadn't reacted yet. It lay on the ground exactly as it had been standing. The roach's snakelike tongue hung mid-arch and its mouth was still contorted into that same curse.

I aimed my shovel at the roach's face and took a deep breath.

Seconds later, time resumed. The roach had no idea what hit him. He looked up at me in confusion just as I brought the shovel onto his face with a sickening crack.

The insect demon screeched in agony.

"Oh, damn!" Bo said. “What the hell happened?”

I didn’t look at the dead man. Instead, I raised my shovel again and brought it down in the same spot on the roach demon's face. The demon instinctively raised his sword to protect itself. I slammed its hands with the shovel, knocking away the sword.

"That’s for invading my house," I said. I brought the shovel down one more time and the roach screamed. A flock of birds flapped furiously out of a nearby tree.

The roach's brain finally caught up with reality. I raised the shovel again but locked it in baseball bat position. Harris and Bo joined me, both pointing their guns at the roach.

"Start talking," I said.

The roach put his hands up like a coward. "I only serve my master,” he said quickly, like a frightened child.

"Who do you serve?" I asked.

"His New Majesty Natkaal," the roach said. "I was just following orders!"

"Which were?" I asked, tightening my grip on the shovel.

"Please! I am in pain, human!"

I brought the shovel down again on the roach's chocolate-colored topmost arm. The demon let out an audible gasp, tilted its head back and roared.

"How about we stop beating around the bush," I said coldly. "I've lost all patience with your kind."

"His New Majesty sent me to spy—no more, no less!"

"Much better," I said.

"Your wards had a weakness that we exploited," the roach demon said. "I could listen, but I could not engage. I telegraphed your location and conversations to my master. How do you think that woman found you at the pancake house? Why else would a roach be on your shoulder at the hospital? Yes, it was me. But at no point could I ever intend you harm. You must know that, necromancer. My master willed it. I was going to apologize before you blew me out of your damned house!"

"A demon apologizing?" I asked. "Sheeeeet…Obviously, you're lying."

"What did the grasshopper want?" Harris asked.

The roach eyed the boyish detective with disgust and spat on the ground. "This does not concern you, meddlesome detective—"

I readied the shovel for another swing.

The roach whimpered. "Okay, I apologize!"

"You have manners," I said sarcastically. "You're surprising me more every minute."

"We are looking for the Lich King. This did not involve you."

"I haven't seen Halgeron," I said. "What makes you think he would come here?"

"My master had a hunch," the roach said.

"His hunch was wrong."

"Very well. May I leave?"

I hadn't considered that. Either I killed this demon where he lay, or he would escape into the world of the living.

I hesitated. The roach sensed it. In an instant, a wet, hot tongue slapped me in the face and knocked the guns out of Bo's and Harris's hands. A sharp insect leg struck me in the chest and sent me halfway across my backyard. I crashed into a mound of dirt.

"You will pay for this!" the roach cried. He scooped up his sword. His tongue flailed all about his body and threw saliva like it had a mind of its own. "You dare threaten me, the great Katsaroth! Oh, this is rich, human."

His wings beat against his body angrily. They sounded like a turbojet ready to take off. I tried to stand, but the vicious wind from the insect demon's wings pushed me back, blowing my clothes all about.

Katsaroth lifted several feet in the air. "If only I had orders to kill you!" he cried. "There is still time. Even if master tells me not to, it will be worth disobeying him just to have your head as a trophy."

His serpentine tongue coiled on itself and slurped across his face. "But that must wait."

Something stopped the roach in mid-conversation. It did a quarter turn, glanced in the direction of Granny's house toward her back porch. The windows of the porch were covered in thick white curtains…except for one. A liver-spotted hand quickly drew a curtain over the window.

I cursed under my breath.

The roach grinned devilishly. "Ah, the nosy neighbor!"

I yelled as Katsaroth buzzed to Granny's porch, broke the window with the hilt of his jagged sword, pulled out Granny by the nape of her floral smock, and dragged her across the yard.

Bo took off running after the roach. The dead man sprang

over my fence and into Granny's yard. Harris and I ran after him, but Bo was faster.

In a flash, Bo grabbed on to the roach's hindlegs, pulling it down.

"Let me go, you brute!" Katsaroth cried.

"I'll let her go when you do, dog!" Bo said. He waved his gun and took aim at Katsaroth.

The roach yelled and slapped the gun out of Bo's hand. Granny looked down at the dead man and at the roach and screamed.

A gunshot cracked. Harris.

The bullet whistled past Katsaroth and the demon barrel-rolled away as Harris let off another shot. The second bullet just missed the roach's wing.

"I'm not telling you again," Bo shouted, yanking on the roach. "Let her go!"

Katsaroth steered toward a tree.

Wham!

The roach flew through the branches. A limb smacked Bo in the face and he let go, crashing onto the ground.

"Help!" Granny cried, reaching for Bo.

"I'm coming, Mrs. Powell!" Bo said, taking in another run. But he didn't make it.

Harris and I caught up to Bo just as Katsaroth buzzed out of the yard. The insect demon flew over a rooftop before he shrank high into the sky.

Granny screamed and flailed her arms until a cloud swallowed her.

CHAPTER TWENTY-TWO

My rage gave way to fear as we parked in the hospital parking garage, ran through a breezeway, and rode the elevator to Kay's floor. All I could think of was Granny and her frightened scream as the roach demon carried her into the clouds.

It was my fault. Again. My batting average lately was terrible. If something happened to Josephine Powell, I would never forgive myself for it. Seeing as Granny was my mother's best friend, my mother wouldn't forgive me for it either.

I had made a miscalculation, and because of my mistake, the roach carried Granny off to God-knows-where. Not to mention I had a giant roach demon-sized hole in my kitchen wall and back porch. I'd had to call my neighbor Ant'ny and ask him for a favor to put up boards and plastic wrap until I got home. He also made sure Hazel stayed inside the house. After that, I was really seething.

We found Kay sitting up in her hospital bed, still handcuffed to a rail. Her auburn hair was still a disheveled mess. Despite the swelling on her busted lip being much improved, she still looked miserable.

A police officer sat next to the bed, monitoring her closely as she ate a meal with one hand free. The meal didn't look appetizing: it was a flabby hospital pork chop, a cup of sad green Jell-O, and a mini carton of skim milk. A heart rate monitor next to the bed traced a calm heart rate on a black background and beeped at regular intervals. The amateur necromancer looked up at us in mid-chew.

Harris nodded to the officer, who left us alone.

"What happened?" she said with a mouthful of food as we surrounded the bed. I stood at the foot.

"You said we could trust you, right?" I asked.

Kay swallowed and wiped a speck of grease from her mouth. She stared at me with those defiant brown eyes. "I told you everything."

"Everything?" Bo asked, his voice quizzical.

We stared at her, letting the silence sink in. The corners of her mouth drooped into a slight frown.

"You forgot one thing," Harris said.

Kay's eyes widened.

"I didn't—"

"When were you going to tell us about the gigantic roach demon that you and your husband let into this world?" I asked.

Silence. The words sank in as Kay looked frantically between us. We'd caught her in her omission.

"Shit."

"Natkaal didn't kill Johnny," I said. "It was the roach, wasn't it? I had assumed it was the grasshopper, but you didn't contradict me. You lied to me."

Kay didn't meet my eyes.

"That's a pretty major detail to leave out, isn't it, Detective Harris?" I asked.

Harris nodded grimly. "That eliminates any chance of a plea bargain. I think I'll have the judge throw the book at you."

"You aren't an attorney!" Kay barked. Her face was ferocious now. Everything she told us before had been an act. Part of my heart broke.

"In any case, you might as well get used to the thought of spending a long time in jail because any chance you had of a sweetheart deal is gone," the boyish detective said with all the authority he could muster.

"What makes you think I'll spend any time behind bars?" she asked. "What makes you think my master won't come for me?"

"He's done with you," I said. "He played you like a cheap flea market fiddle."

"We did a deal in blood!"

"Means nothing," Bo said. "Those insects will do anything to get *you* to do anything, chick."

"Oh, really? I'll prove it to you, dead man."

We waited. Kay tipped her head at the ceiling and shouted at the top of her lungs. The intensity of her scream made me jump back.

"Master!" she cried. "I need you now! You name your terms, and I will obey. I don't care what they are. Rid me of these fools so I can be with my Johnny!"

The speech winded her and she panted. The officer poked his head into the room, looking alarmed. "What is it now?"

Harris gave the man a friendly wave and a nod to please excuse us. The officer left, still on edge. I didn't envy him having to watch Kay every second.

Kay looked between us and then around the hospital room, incredulous that her request had gone unanswered.

"No," she breathed.

"Natkaal used you for lightcraft," I said. "He got a few uses of the spell for free. Knowing what I know about demons, he's going to let you rot in jail. Quite frankly, you deserve it."

I motioned to Bo and Harris and we started to leave.

"Wait," she said. "You're not going to ask me where Natkaal might be?"

"You don't know," I said, not turning around. "I'll get my information the old-fashioned way from now on."

"And what's that?" she asked.

I wiggled my jacket pocket and the razor blade jingled inside. "I tried to warn you, Kay. It seems you've made your choice."

A flicker of guilt flashed in her eyes, but she averted her gaze. Somewhere deep inside her was a conscience. I wasn't sure it would ever regain a foothold.

She was silent as we left her.

CHAPTER TWENTY-THREE

HARRIS, Bo, and I huddled in the hospital hallway. We waited for a trio of nurses to pass before we started. The officer who had been watching Kay was finishing up making a coffee nearby.

"What now?" Bo asked.

"Step two of your plan," I said.

"Bet," Bo said, fist bumping me.

"We'll head to the spirit world," I said. "I want answers straight from the source."

"There's only one problem," Harris said. "We're not exactly in private around here."

I glanced up and down the corridor. Nurses and doctors moved around here and there. Somewhere, a patient was yelling curse words.

I nodded and parted the curtain to Kay's room. Bo and Harris followed me in.

Kay was sulking on her hospital bed. Upon seeing me, her face brightened. Before she could open her mouth, I said, "We are not here for you."

Before the amateur necromancer could respond, I had my razor blade in hand. I made a quick cut on my palm and envisioned the smoky spirit world stretching before me. A ragged stitch of light illuminated the room with cool blue tones.

Whatever Kay said, I didn't hear it because we had already passed into the spirit world.

Mist settled around us as the stitch closed. A wall of sulfur and smoke hit my nostrils. It had been a while since I had been here, but the smell always hit me the same. In the sky, a phantom whistled overhead like a mad firework before exploding into a soul-screaming pop. Ahead stretched an endless flatland of dead grass, and rocks. Fingers of mist gathered over this place like a hand closing over a throat.

We couldn't see very well. It was smokier than usual.

I knew the area. We were near CeCe's lake. I waited for her to appear.

She didn't.

We walked for a while in the ragged mist, not saying anything. The gentle breeze blew, parting the mist somewhat. A few yards away, golden light twinkled among the grass and rocks.

A lich lake. All three of us saw it at the same time. We stalked through the mist toward it, entranced by gentle dazzles of sparkles lighting just under the surface. They flickered like candles against a diaphanous shade.

Normally, when I called the dead, I did it from the safety of my own home in a magic circle. It was more convenient. I didn't have to worry about making cuts on my palm. Sure, you had to occasionally worry about accidentally snagging a demon into your circle, and sure, demons could be awfully problematic, but it was safer.

Here, you could go straight to the source—straight to the surface of the lich lakes where the dead slumbered, marinating in lich water as they contemplated their ascent to the next plane of existence. You just had to make a deal with a lich, and you could stay as long as you wanted, get whatever answers you needed. There was always the possibility of a rogue demon attack, but they weren't as bold here, not with liches roaming around.

Demons and liches didn't mix. Maybe that was why the grand universe put them side by side here in the spirit world on top of each other. It ensured peace.

The current cloud of mist broke, and there we were, standing on the shore of an enormous lake with placid waters. The golden cores of thousands of souls swirled in the depths like strange fish, and there was the faint jingling of what sounded like wind chimes somewhere over the lake.

Where was CeCe? She should have appeared by now. Any time I showed up in the spirit world, she was all too happy to see me. She had a habit of appearing right next to me when I least expected it.

I knelt and dipped a hand in the water. Rather, I *tried* to dip a hand in the water. A film of electric blue energy sprang up over the surface of the lake like a net of plasma. Symmetrical and exotic-looking crimson runes appeared everywhere. My fingers tingled with a strange buzzing sensation before I jerked them out of the water.

It was a ward.

Bo scratched his head. "Aw, man. Remember what CeCe told us?"

I stood, wincing as my knees popped.

"She said the lakes were closed until further notice," the dead man said. "Something about the liches looking for Halgeron. We forgot about that. Sorry, boss man."

I cursed under my breath.

CeCe *had* come to warn us. She hadn't been kidding.

"So she's off looking for the king?" Harris asked. He put his hands on his hips and glanced all around the spirit world. "Where do you think the big skull went?"

"Halgeron will be Halgeron," I said. "But I don't have time for this. I've got to find Granny."

"Well," Bo said, "so much for step two."

I paced back and forth along the jagged rocks of the lake, thinking. The answers to all my problems were right here in the water, but they might as well have been miles away. And then I became aware of the paper bag in my interior coat pocket resting against my chest. The suncatcher.

I had an idea.

"Not again," Bo said. "You already took a few minutes off your life, man."

"Gonna need a few minutes more," I said.

Mentally, I tracked through all the steps in the spell again. I called up that great enmity against Natkaal. I held the grasshopper in my mind's eye as I wished nothing more than to stop him from pulling off whatever dastardly plan he had cooking. It dawned on me that if I wanted, I could find him down here. I could hunt the bug and end it right now on my terms. But that would have been unwise. He would have no doubt anticipated that. And if he was the new supernatural sheriff in town, he'd have plenty of his insect friends with him.

No. I didn't care about the grasshopper right now. All I cared about was Granny. I held her face in my mind's eye too.

"Lester Broussard, you need a good lawyer," she said, wagging her fingers at me. Granny's face morphed into a motherly scowl. "Don't be stubborn about this."

Now, she was in my kitchen with a plate of peach cobbler, telling me she told me so. And then I was a boy again, nine years old, with a bag of tomatoes in my hand, sent by my mother to take to Granny. My mother had a garden in the backyard and the plants always bore so much fruit that we couldn't eat them all. I'd ring the doorbell at Granny's front door and trade a sack of tomatoes for a bag of sugar. She'd answer the door, ask me "how are you doing baby", and tell me to come inside. She always had a Bible verse she was working on memorizing, and she made sure to tell me about it. All these years later, the verses escaped me, but a smile settled on my face as I thought about those warm moments in her foyer.

You should have seen Granny and my mother together. They were a gossiping, laughing bunch. Laughter somewhere, from a balmy moonlit night, drifted from a distant memory back to me now as I held all these memories in my mind's eye. I just wanted to bring Granny home.

The feelings swelled to a critical mass and I knew the shadowcraft spell was materializing around me.

There were no clouds or storms or walls of soundless fury down here. The spirit world had enough energy all its own. It was easier to cast shadowcraft down here because the place was filled with—well, you know, shadows.

My gut of guts told me that the spell had taken hold.

I held the suncatcher up to the light. Except there was no light down here either. No sun. But that didn't matter. I willed all of my intent into the suncatcher, thinking of Natkaal and Granny and the roach demon and Harris and Bo and even Orman Misterka. I let my thoughts wander, let them all flow into the magical piece of glass wedged in my palm.

Warmth radiated from the glass and across my skin. The suncatcher exploded into a solar flare of light. Everything in my world flashed yellow and white. It took every ounce of energy I had not to let go of the glass.

The lightcraft had been activated.

I remembered what Camille told me, how lightcraft could help you find what you had lost. Now I thought only of Granny. My consciousness zoomed upward into the light, and suddenly, I was everywhere all at once.

The vast and infinite lakes of the spirit world stretched in front and underneath me as if I were flying over them and walking across them at the same time. This place truly was a land of lakes. The dead lands were dull continents among all the gold and sparkling.

My consciousness tilted as if on a z-axis and the world tipped up slightly so I could see underneath it, into the depths of the lakes at another angle. They had no end. The translucent water hung down into an infinite blackness that knew no bottom. Souls streamed all the way down. The very thought terrified me. All the ancestors of antiquity blazed far, far in the deeps.

The spirit world shifted on its z-axis again. Or maybe I shifted. Now I was looking up at the world of the living, like a lazy beach traveler lying on the sand and gazing up at the sky. The vastness of the world drifted by like herds of cumulus clouds on a windy day. Mountainous terrains, oceans, barren deserts, and lush green forests and jungles floated by as I took in a long inhale. The sound of five billion voices chattered in my head, saying nothing and everything all at once. And then I realized that the world of the living was growing larger, magnifying as if a cosmic hand were dialing in the zoom ring on a microscope ever so slowly.

North America crept up on me, surrounded at first by the jeweled blue Atlantic and Pacific oceans. Then it was all brown, city-marked land. Suburbs and suburbs and suburbs sprawled out here and there like little tribal designs. The faint lines of a map insinuated themselves against the landscape. I knew them as the Missouri state lines. My vision zoomed toward the little knob on the eastern side of the state, that great knob illuminated by the dark brown, muddy waters of the Mississippi River.

The Mississippi River carved a sharp line between the skyscrapered, crowded terrain of downtown and the more spread-out city blocks of East St. Louis. And of course, my city's arch was there too, glinting like a shiny staple along the muddy banks.

I was in my city now, zooming fast. A golden tint sprang up around the skyscrapers of downtown.

I recognized some of the buildings. Some were downtown landmarks with unmistakable rooftops and spires. Rivers of traffic inched through the narrow downtown streets.

My vision tilted, fanning me out west, away from downtown. Now I was high over the sky, but close enough to see every detail of the rooftops—the tar and gravel roofs, the rooftop air conditioners sitting silent in winter slumber, and the blinking lights of a satellite tower here and there.

The white noise of the city enveloped me. I was one with the cars speeding down the streets, the gaggles of pigeons hooting as they fluttered away across rooftops, and the airplanes easing across the sky.

I inhaled as I took in the oneness with my great city. My vision zoomed in so fast that had I been there, it would have rattled my skull and pulled the skin on my face back with G force.

I should've been losing my mind right now. No one—and I mean no one—was meant to travel this quickly. But that was the way of strange magic.

Once, I had become a reaper for a day. I could warp anywhere in the world with a single thought. Back then, my body had popped in and out of existence as I pleased. I channeled my inner reaper and just let it be. No thinking, no worrying, just pure existence.

I was headed toward a cluster of gray buildings now. A complex of some sort. It looked important. It stood tall, towering over office and masonry buildings. Beacons blinked on the roofs.

A helipad with bright white bands and a giant "H" caught my eye. The edges of the circle were ringed with snow.

Was I heading for…a helipad?

My vision narrowed to a single point in the center of the

helipad. A dark shape. I inhaled one more time as my vision narrowed, discerning the shape in the snow.

The shape was a pattern of blue, red, and purple. A patterned print of some kind.

Atop the floral pattern blew a tangle of gray in the winter breeze. Hair.

A person was sitting on the helipad. I saw them clearly now. Floral smock. Silver curls. It was still.

Every muscle in my body tensed as Granny sharpened into view. She sat dead center in the middle of the helipad, sitting freely in a plastic chair. Her head slumped onto her chest, but she was breathing.

My vision slammed to a stop. Granny's body lit up in a column of golden light. My vision blinked around her like a camera taking pictures at different angles. The exercise burned the images into my mind's eye. Then it zoomed out and showed me the building from various distances at all angles—north, south, east, and west.

I knew the tall mixture of mortar, brick, and glass outright. I knew the red-covered canopy on the first floor with white letters on it. I knew the trio of parking garages cater-cornered to each other. And I knew the parking lot, for my Lincoln Town Car was currently parked on the third floor.

Granny was at the hospital.

CHAPTER TWENTY-FOUR

My vision hung on Granny for a few moments longer to ensure I knew her location. The shimmering pillar of light that enveloped her expanded outward. The light smoothed over like hands over a satin blanket. Soon, the entire hospital was a golden pillar of light.

Then, an invisible hand levered shutters on a window closed, and I saw nothing. The vision was dark, and only when I realized how dark it was did I feel my eyes were closed. They had been closed this entire time, but I saw as if they were open.

I opened my eyes. Speckles of golden light flooded around me before the fetid air of this place carried them over the surface of CeCe's lake and extinguished them.

A hand touched my shoulder. Bo. I startled at the sight of the dead man. The effects of the lightcraft were still strong in my body. I wasn't used to being back in reality yet.

"You all right?" Bo asked. "What did you see, boss man?"

"She's on the roof of the hospital," I said.

"Get out of here," Harris said.

"She's there. She's going to get hypothermia if we don't get to her as soon as possible."

A warm wind blew, and I sensed that we weren't alone.

I froze. A ring of shadows surrounded us, shrouded by the mist. A quiet breeze tugged a finger of mist aside, and I spotted the red and yellow insectoid eyes.

Quiet laughter began in the ring and drifted to us as dozens of insect demons stepped forward.

There were too many to count. I had never seen any of them before. Each was more garish than the last.

There was a giant humpback spider with only one fang and hairy human arms growing from the top of its abdomen. A fuzzy caterpillar stood as tall as a giraffe, covered in wavering silver hair and pus-filled eyes that ran down the length of its thorax. Next to it was a katydid whose paperlike shell was so translucent, I could spot the veins of blue blood coursing through its body.

There were so many demons, it made my head spin.

Bo, Harris, and I retreated toward each other, standing shoulder to shoulder and back to back as the unruly gang closed in. The insect demons laughed and snickered and cursed at me in their brutal, consonant-heavy murderous tongue.

"Where's a can of bug spray when you need it?" Bo asked, pulling out his gun.

"They don't make cans big enough for these guys," I said.

"No, we just need a nuclear bomb," Harris said.

"Joke all you want, pathetic humans," one of the insects rasped. "It won't do you any good now."

They had us completely circled. We couldn't run even if we wanted to. If I cut a hole to the world of the living, they would follow us back, and I would be responsible for unleashing the horde upon humanity.

The insect demons closed the circle with a few quick paces. Their movement was hurried and coordinated.

Somewhere, a horn sounded, followed by a sniveling voice.

"Bow your heads for His New Majesty, the king of demons!"

Instantly, every insect had a weapon in his hand. They extended them outward, letting us know they really meant business. Then they knelt and bowed their heads. A few feet ahead, the ground shook and buzz saws appeared, tracing a narrow circle into the rocks and dirt. The saws whined and threw up rainbow-colored sparks. The earth collapsed, dirt and rocks tumbling far below. The ground rumbled again as something rose from the hole.

The first thing I saw was a golden crown. Rubies, emeralds, and sapphires gleamed against a frame of pure gold. It was the kind of crown you saw in cartoons, with pointy edges. It was askew. Of course, Natkaal was wearing it.

The grasshopper sat perched on a palanquin carried by two ant demons. The palanquin was brocaded and covered with a gaudy red and silver rug. The grasshopper looked bored, staring at the nails on his human hands. His body was a deep viridian that reminded me of the inner depths of an evil forest. Upon seeing me, Harris, and Bo, the grasshopper demon grinned.

"Welcome to the neighborhood!" he cried. "You have the privilege and honor of being the first royal guests in my court."

"And probably the only guests you'll ever get," I said.

The insect demons rose. They kept their weapons pointed at us. The tension in the air grew palpable. If someone had lit a match, the place would have exploded.

Something tapped me on the shoulder. I turned just as a white fist clocked me in the jaw. I was on the ground before I knew it. Soon, Bo and Harris landed next to me.

Kay stood over me, shaking out her fist. She was still in her hospital gown. The roach demon stood next to her, laughing like a maniac.

"You thought I was going to jail," Kay said. "You're really hard-headed."

"You better believe it," I said, sitting up.

"Now that we have gotten the prefatory matters out of the way," Natkaal said, "this is the part where I warn you again about my power, Lester. Do you understand your ineptitude before me yet? For every ounce of guile you have, I have ten times more. You haven't even seen my true power."

I stood up, panting. My face was raw from where Kay punched me. She was going to leave a bruise.

"I'm prepared to go all night," I said.

"So are we," a female voice said.

CeCe had materialized behind Natkaal with her rose-gold sword leveled at the grasshopper demon, inches from his head. The grasshopper gave a startled yelp at the sight of her. Then, upon realizing she was alone, he gave his horse whinny laugh.

"You're alone, lich! We outnumber you. For threatening regicide, I will find your phylactery and shatter it into a trillion pieces!"

CeCe's platinum hair and scarlet dress rippled in the breeze. She tilted her head and gave a sarcastic smile. "My dear grasshopper, what makes you think I would be so stupid as to be alone?"

Natkaal's eyes widened. In an instant, dark shapes spawned all around us, followed by the metallic whine of swords being drawn from their scabbards. An army of pale-faced men and women leveled their swords at the demons. The women wore couture dresses like CeCe's, with spikes on the shoulders. The men wore untucked dress shirts and capes that blew wildly behind them. There was a lich for every demon.

The demons had their weapons at the throats of Bo, Harris, and me, and the liches had their swords pointed at the demons. It was a supernatural standoff.

"You alabaster idiot!" Natkaal cried at CeCe. The

grasshopper jumped up and down on his palanquin again. His ant servants strained and groaned with each jump. "All of this could have been avoided if your cowardly king had listened to my demands!"

"All of this could have been avoided if you had just minded your business," CeCe said. "Besides, you were never going to join forces with Halgeron anyway."

The grasshopper regarded the comment, then shrugged. "I'm a demon. Do you ever expect me to keep my word?"

"Then how do you ever expect us to trust you?" CeCe asked. "You don't want a partnership. You want Halgeron's phylactery."

My friend's face hardened. "Or, you found it, didn't you?"

Natkaal grinned as if to say, "I'm not telling."

Liches were immortal. You could kill one dead, but it would always reanimate. To truly kill a lich, you have to find its phylactery. The rumor on the street was that liches put their souls in jars, but I never believed that. Liches went to great lengths to protect their phylacteries, for if you destroyed it, you destroyed the lich's soul forever.

I had never given much thought to Halgeron's phylactery. The Lich King used strong magic that likely hid it well.

"What do you want with Halgeron's phylactery?" I asked.

"What anyone would want with the Lich King's soul," Natkaal said. He lay on the palanquin and the ants spawned palm fronds and blew fetid air at him feverishly. "The archdemons have been doing things the wrong way for the last thousand years, and I intend to let them know in no uncertain terms."

"Whatever happened to respecting your elders?" I asked, thinking of the archdemons. I had killed one who would not have been pleased to hear Natkaal speaking of his demonic elders in this way.

"I want to be an archdemon," Natkaal said. "I want to ascend. To do that, I must do something big and bold, something that has never been done before. Bigger, better, faster—"

"Harder, stronger, blah blah blah," Bo said, twirling his finger and telling Natkaal to hurry up.

The grasshopper growled at him. "You get the idea. Unlike the rest of my brethren, I am intelligent."

"Humility, much?" CeCe asked.

"Truth," Natkaal said. "I'm simply saying what has needed to be said for a thousand years, lich. I won't be denied. If I can find the Lich King's phylactery and destroy it, then I become the de facto king of the spirit world. I would preside over two dominions—lich and demon. Wouldn't that be grand? Fate will not deny me, so you would do well to watch your tongue. You will soon be bowing to me."

This definitely wasn't the grasshopper I knew. The Natkaal I knew didn't make such outlandish schemes. He definitely wouldn't have announced them to the world. There had to be something about this plan that he wasn't telling me. The pomposity had to be a front.

"What happens if you don't find the phylactery?" I asked. "What if we stop you? And why tip your hand so soon? Now everybody knows you're after Halgeron's soul jar. When Halgeron comes back around, do you think he's going to be happy?"

"I anticipated your question," Natkaal said seriously. "I read about this in a self-help book."

A worn hardcover book appeared in one of his human hands. The hand leafed through it, and he studied the text thoughtfully. "Here it is, though it is worded quite inelegantly. I'll paraphrase a human saying that I agree with for a change: when you verbalize your intent, the entire universe conspires to help you achieve it."

He chucked the book, and it bounced across the dirt before vanishing in a wisp of smoke.

"My time among humans was most educational, necromancer. I have you to thank for that, and I am in your eternal debt. If my blood weren't running through your veins, and if killing you wouldn't also kill me, I would allow you a quick death."

"I'm touched," I said flatly. "But here's what I think. You're just trying to get a rise out of us. Maybe you want Halgeron's phylactery, maybe you don't. But that's not your true goal."

The grasshopper threw his head back and laughed. "You're catching on! In another thousand years, you will have figured out my plan, Lester Broussard. But for now, we dance."

I took a step forward and the demons warned me to stop. The blade of a scimitar poked at my Adam's apple.

I stared at Natkaal defiantly. "I thought about our last conversation," I said. With one hand, I pushed the scimitar side and shoved my way past a caterpillar demon.

All the demons chattered at once, barking at me, but they didn't move.

I knew they wouldn't touch me. They would go after Harris next, but they couldn't do that, because if they did, the liches would get them.

Kay held the suncatcher high into the sky. "Stay back!"

I ignored her. "Here's how this is going to go down," I said. "You leave Granny, Harris, and other innocents out of this. If anything happens to Granny on that roof, you will be sorry."

"She is merely collateral damage," Natkaal snarled. The grasshopper demon leaned off the palanquin and met my face. He stopped inches away from mine.

Storm clouds brewed above out of nowhere. It set the sky phantoms into an anxious fury. They popped like a fireworks display.

Natkaal grinned at me. Then, the grasshopper was gone.

One second, he'd been there grinning at me. The next, he and all the other demons were gone.

My heart raced as I glanced around. The liches also looked around frantically before sheathing their swords.

In an instant, CeCe stood next to me. "I knew you'd come back," she said with a long face. Normally, she was happy to see me; now her face was haggard and tired. "Sorry it had to be under these circumstances."

"Where the hell is Natkaal?" I asked.

"Lightcraft," Bo said. "When Kay held up that suncatcher, she initiated a spell."

"Where do you think they went?" Harris asked.

CeCe shrugged. "My guess is that they probably found Halgeron. And we have no idea where to start."

I nodded to CeCe. "We'll help you find Halgeron, but I've got to take care of some business first."

I imagined the physical world. The hospital helipad appeared in a jagged stitch before me.

Bo, Harris, and I jumped through the stitch to rescue Granny.

CHAPTER TWENTY-FIVE

JUMPING from the spirit world back into wintry St. Louis was a shock to the senses. A wall of frigid wind slammed into me as I landed on the helipad.

The air here was crisp and frostbitten. I didn't miss the sulfuric, smoky smell of the spirit world one bit.

The sky was ribboned with white and gray. Even though it could've qualified as a heat wave today, I still shivered and hugged myself as the ragged stitch closed behind us.

Granny sat in a chair in the middle of the helipad, her head slumped down. A bitter wind blew almost out of nowhere and whipped her floral smock about. The old woman was in a sorry state. The demon had just thrown her in a chair and left her for dead.

I ran to her and took her hands. Her skin was icy and her pulse was weak. She shivered terribly.

"Granny," I said quietly.

"I'll call the hospital and have someone up here immediately," Harris said, sliding his phone out of his pocket. He dialed 911.

"This is Detective Damian Harris. I need urgent assistance..."

I tapped one of Granny's cheeks and said her name again.

"Granny, it's me, Lester. Everything's going to be all right. We're at the hospital and you're going to get the care that you need. Granny. Granny?"

The old woman stirred again. She mumbled something about the Lord taking her. It broke my heart.

"I am not at liberty to share how I got up here," Harris said. "I need a medical team. I've got an elderly woman suffering from hypothermia. What? No. Like I said, it doesn't matter how I got up here."

Bo bent down and said, "Mrs. Powell, I promise we won't let anything else happen to you."

Suddenly, the old woman opened her eyes. Bo was the first thing she saw. She startled at the sight of the dead man.

"Conserve your strength," I said softly. I called Harris's name and hooked my thumb at Granny.

Harris spoke more forcefully into his phone. "Yes, I know there isn't a helicopter up here and that this sounds weird. Oh, for Christ's sake, I'm *not* trespassing. Listen to me: if I don't get a medical team up here now, I'm going to have someone's ass!"

Granny's eyes locked on Bo. "You," she said, slurring her words. "You…fought…that thing."

She was recalling the fight with the roach. I sure didn't want to think about it.

"We got a lot of catching up to do, Mrs. Powell," Bo said, taking off his sunglasses. Granny looked into his deep, dark, and dead eyes and mumbled something that we didn't understand.

I didn't have time to ask her to clarify. Seconds later, an automatic door nearby whistled open.

Bo, Harris, and I watched as a team of paramedics wheeled a stretcher onto the roof, loaded Granny onto it, and whisked her deep into the bowels of the hospital.

I was trembling. If anything happened to Granny, it would

be my fault. She wouldn't have been the only casualty either. My ire rose for the roach demon. Whoever could do this to an old woman didn't have a heart. They weren't qualified to walk this earth—or any world as far as I was concerned. I tried not to let rage consume me. I pushed the tongue-lashing brute out of my mind.

"She's gonna be all right, boss man," Bo said, patting my shoulder.

"She shouldn't have been here in the first place," I said.

I needed a minute. I stared up at the dramatic ribboned sky, wishing that I had the spiritual toolkit to address how I was feeling. I didn't know if it would help, but it certainly couldn't hurt to get down on my knees and ask God for some kind of favor—any kind of favor. Granny's children, grandchildren, and great-grandchildren were depending on it.

The hospital admitted Granny. She was suffering from hypothermia. A grim-faced doctor told me that she was lucky to be alive. Another few minutes and her body would have shut down. The nurses wrapped her in thermal blankets, gave her fluids in an IV to help replenish electrolytes, and started a process called rewarming. The doctor's technical explanations were lost on me. All I cared about was that her prognosis looked to be good. I shook the doctor's hand with a sigh of gratitude.

It was a relief to hear him tell me that Granny would pull through, but it wasn't a relief to call Granny's son and tell him and the family to get to the hospital ASAP because there had been an accident.

What *was* I going to tell them? I didn't know. Then again, it wasn't my place. Nobody knew how she ended up on the hospital roof. Maybe it was better that way.

"Say, Doctor," I said. "I was here earlier and I stumbled

upon the hospital chapel. Can you tell me where I might find it?"

The doctor pointed to the elevator and gave me directions.

I held the laughing chaplain's face in my mind's eye. I remembered how she had laughed with me in the hospital room, how she had educated Bo and me on the merits of stained glass.

I left Bo and Harris standing like sentinels outside Granny's room. Heaven help any supernatural creature that messed with them.

I stopped in a canteen and made myself a cup of cheap coffee. It was black and bland, just what I needed. I reached for hazelnut creamer and sugar to make the taste more bearable, but I got it in my head that maybe a little bit of suffering would do me some good. Maybe it would make my prayers go a little further.

I sipped the black and earthy coffee as an elevator inched down and deposited me onto the pediatric floor. Vibrant azure wallpaper, stickers of Disney characters surrounded by sparkles, and positive affirmations greeted me as I walked down the hallway, remembering the doctor's instructions.

This path didn't seem familiar. I reached the end of the long corridor that the doctor told me was sure to test my legs, then I turned left.

The hospital chapel was a cozy room with frosted double doors tucked at the end of the hall. The word "Chapel" was stenciled quietly on the glass. You couldn't have missed the interfaith symbols painted on the wall and the sandwich board on the carpet advertising in pastel colors that all were welcome. The chapel wanted you to know it was here.

I stopped with my coffee blazing in my hand and stared at the doors. This must have been a different entrance. Confused, I opened the door.

The chapel was a stuffy, windowless room packed with wooden pews organized in a diagonal slant toward a lectern at the front of the room. Behind the lectern was an oil painting of a sun and moon intermixed with each other in dramatic golds, silvers, and purples. The walls almost completely blocked out the hustle and bustle from the hospital outside.

I stood stunned, taking in the place. A petite Indian woman passed a vacuum down one of the aisles. The tiny motor droned like an angry hornet. Upon seeing me, the woman shut off the vacuum and apologized.

"Excuse me," I said. “Where is the other chapel?"

The woman stared at me for a moment. At first, I thought she didn’t speak English. Her response was slow. "This is it, sir."

I surveyed the room. "I think there's a misunderstanding.” I said it more for myself than for her. "I was in the chapel not too long ago. It was a dark room with a beautiful stained-glass window."

"Perhaps it was the other building?" the woman asked. “There is an interfaith service there too."

"No, it was this one," I said insistently. "Now that I’m thinking about it, it was between Psychiatry and Cardiology."

The Indian woman looked at me like I was certifiably crazy. "I'm sorry, sir, but there is no chapel there. Would you like me to leave you alone?"

The words hit me. Hard.

There was only one chapel? How could there be only one chapel?

My knees were weak as I contemplated the gravity of what she told me. Through the padded walls, a distant paging system chimed and a muffled voice called a doctor’s name.

I excused myself and walked toward the door. Before I opened it, I turned to the woman and said, "Let me ask you one more question. I spoke with the hospital chaplain. Black woman. Beige business suit, dreadlocks, ruby stud earrings. She laughed a lot. Did I imagine her?"

"We have a chaplain team here," the woman said, pointing

to a wall of photos. "But I don't think any match that description, sir."

I studied the photos. The wood frame portraits on the wall were what you expected a team of hospital chaplains to look like—kind, smiling, and warm. There wasn't a black woman among them.

I took in the photos for a moment, thanked the woman for her time and let myself out.

I walked down the antiseptic hospital corridor as if in a daze. Just what the hell was going on? All I had wanted to do was pray. I could barely do that.

Maybe it was true that I couldn't go back to the stained-glass room, but sure, I could pray. I didn't need a chapel to do it.

I found an empty waiting room. I had no idea where I was, and I didn't care. I sat in a plush chair under an oil painting of two ducks on a pond, and I closed my eyes.

You see, I've never been a man of prayer. When Amira received her cancer diagnosis, I had prayed to the big man upstairs, tried to bargain with him. Nothing happened. I don't know why, but ever since then, I always felt like I had to take things into my own hands, like there was no one in this world that was going to swoop in and save me.

I saved my wife from cancer with the dark art, with my own damn hands. I solved my own problem, found my own solution out of seeming nothingness. That solution had been poisoned. I got my wife back, but I lost her shortly after. But I had gotten her back. As far as the cosmos were concerned, I was one of the luckiest men in the history of existence. Who else could say they got to spend more time with the woman they loved against all odds? Who else could say that they spat in the eyes of fate and lived to tell about it?

Who else could say that fate had spat back with even more force, taking not only its requested share, but my son as interest?

Even if I had found religion, religion wouldn't have wanted anything to do with me. You could say that we lived at arm's length. Glance back at any of my adventures and prove me otherwise.

And now, here I was, at some sort of cosmic junction. The idea was in my head to pray. I had no idea how it got there, but I acted on it.

I hung my head and closed my eyes. Then it occurred to me that I had no idea how to pray. Surely it wasn't supposed to be like it was in the movies. Surely you weren't supposed to talk out loud. Could you pray in your head? I didn't know.

I thought I might feel something, that I might know what to ask. I had no clue. All I could think of was Granny. I just wanted her to be okay.

I opened my eyes, slightly disoriented. A wave of calm started in my chest and washed downward, but I didn't feel anything else. At least I did it—not for me, but for Granny.

Knowing my luck, Natkaal had already found Halgeron's phylactery. I had to admit that the grasshopper had bested me. No matter what happened, I wouldn't give up. I wouldn't let him win.

I sat there in the waiting room, not saying anything and not thinking much. I took in another oil painting of a lone tree in the middle of a field, standing tall and gnarled in wintry sunlight. Feeling like I could do nothing else, I downed the last of my coffee and headed for the elevator.

Alone in the elevator, I punched the number for Granny's floor. I heard some sort of commotion upstairs. It sounded like people talking loudly and furniture scuffing and scooting across the floor. As the car rose up the shaft, the sounds materialized into screams and yells. They were screams of agony. Someone was crying for help.

Every cell in my body sprang to attention.

Just as the elevator doors opened onto Granny's floor, the lights went out.

CHAPTER TWENTY-SIX

Two heart-pounding seconds of silence and darkness later, the generators cycled on, casting the hospital corridor in a sickly golden and white glow with an eerie B-list horror movie ambiance. I had expected the hospital's generator lights to be brighter, starker, and more clinical so that medical staff could still go about their daily business. I got the feeling that something supernatural was forcing the lights down low.

A wave of human shapes ran through the darkness toward the elevator but stopped upon seeing the power outage. The whites of their eyes shone in the pale light. I maneuvered through the crowd, smelling both cologne and sick. There were patients among the crowd, and medical staff were helping them. God bless the doctors and nurses for being so composed.

One of them was a doctor. I knew her by the metallic stethoscope around her neck that caught the light.

I grabbed the woman's arm. "What's going on?" I asked.

The woman recoiled from me, visibly perturbed. The lights cast strange and harsh shadows over her fearful face. I said a few calm words. Still, she could hardly speak. "There was a—a…I can't believe—"

"What?" I asked.

"I've got to get my patients to safety, sir," she said sternly and apologetically, taking an elderly woman by the hand.

The woman disappeared into the herd, which was rushing toward the stairwell down the hall.

The power outage killed the signs on the ceiling, but the signs' battery backups made them glow with a faint red aura, with the exit signs extra luminous from yards away. I recognized one of the signs and remembered the way to Granny's room. I felt my way through the darkness, stumbling on a gurney here and there. Whatever happened, I had to make sure Granny was okay.

I slowed my breathing, telling myself to keep it together. The slower I breathed, the better I could think, and trust me, it was hard to think right now. Occasionally, I bumped into someone who was moving silently through the hallway, scared out of their wits. I kept thinking that my luck might run out. The next thing I ran into might not be human.

I kept my center of gravity low as I worked my way methodically through the shadows, stopping to listen every few feet. Footfalls were all around me. Labored breaths passed by me as someone ran every now and again. In the rooms, abandoned patients cried for help.

Somewhere, the unmistakable crack of a gunshot intensified the frenzy. I instinctively ducked as more screams ripped across the hospital ward.

"Good grief," I said under my breath, arching my back and creeping toward the direction of the gunshot. I really, really would have felt better with a gun right now.

Cold sweat bloomed all over my body as I thought of the possibility that either Bo or Harris could have fired the gun.

A growling sound stopped me. Every muscle in my body tensed as I caught a whiff of something foul—like putrid breath and brimstone.

The generator lights flickered. Before they went out, I

spotted a row of serrated teeth. Something was perched askew on the wall, grinning at me.

I jumped out of the way just as Katsaroth crashed into the wall near me, making a giant hole and throwing up plaster and dust.

I ran as fast as I could. The roach demon bellowed and I heard him stomping after me. He roared my name with equal parts delight and fury.

"I'm not done with you yet!"

I looked around the darkness. Aside from some chairs, pens, and a clipboard with medical records, I was weaponless.

I ducked as I rounded the corner. The roach demon was unsteady on his feet and crashed into another wall. This time, he didn't break it. He must've recovered quickly because the air grew warm around me as he slashed at me with his tongue.

"I can't kill you, but I can put you in a coma. That would please His New Majesty! It would also solve the dual death problem, don't you think?"

So Katsaroth wasn't as dumb as he looked.

I was sure I passed Granny's room. A quick millisecond glance inside showed that she was sleeping on her bed, covered in thick blankets. I didn’t look again. Apparently, Katsaroth wasn’t interested in her. If he was, he would have stomped into the room and used her as bait to attract me. Despite my heart pounding, I was relieved.

Somewhere, the floor rumbled. A nasally voice roared. Suddenly, the air was electric with buzzing.

Something hard and wet slammed into my back, throwing me to the floor.

Katsaroth wrapped his tongue around me and lifted me into the air. He laughed as he brought me close. His tongue tightened around my jacket as he squeezed.

The roach said something, but with his tongue wrapped around me, he spoke like somebody with a mouthful of food. A wave of his putrid breath made me want to vomit.

The demon whipped me across the corridor and slammed me against a wall, knocking out all my wind. He dragged me up and down the wall as he studied me. He said something else unintelligible—something between a mumble and a gargle. He laughed his stentorian laugh. Demons only laughed like that just before they were about to kill you.

Then, Katsaroth froze. From the corner of my eye, blue lightning flashed at the end of the hall, followed by a low underscore of thunder.

A shaft of golden light cut down from above, straight into the tongue. A second later, I was on the floor. The tongue had slipped off me and clattered to the floor in the same position that it held me.

Katsaroth was frozen in time. He didn't yet realize he had half a tongue.

A throaty dog's bark caught my attention, followed by a furry nuzzle against my leg. I glanced down to see Hazel panting at my side.

"Sweet pea?" I asked, startling.

I looked around. A shadowcraft spell had taken hold. Hazel barked again; leaden walls swallowed the sound.

"Hazel, how did you get here?" I asked.

Nearby, footsteps tracked away. A sparkle of golden light disappeared around the corner. It caught my eye like a sequin on the surface of a lake at dusk, then flashed away.

Hazel whined, subtly telegraphing her fear. I reached down and comforted her.

The door to the stairwell clanged open, followed by hurried steps running up the stairs.

"Come on," I said. Hazel followed me.

Generator lights lit up the stairwell in the same sickly glow as the hallways.

I glanced up the well, between the landings. A trail of golden light spiraled two flights above, followed by the open and slam of another metallic door. Soft golden orbs of light whirled through the air before fading.

I ran as fast as I could, Hazel right on my heels. Two flights later, I pushed onto the next floor. I slid to a stop and let my eyes adjust to the darkness. Hazel crouched next to me. Several yards away, the golden light disappeared around another corner. I raced toward it.

The corridor was a dead end. There were three curtained rooms. A lone window betrayed a wall of furious blue lightning.

I tried to quiet my panting as I crept down the hall.

I parted the first curtain. There was nothing but an empty hospital room, a well-made bed, and a TV.

I crept to the second curtain. I took a deep breath before opening it and poking my head in. An old man was frozen trying to get out of his hospital bed. He was hooked up to a mobile IV. He had cannulas in his nose and looked frightened.

I replaced the curtain and took a final deep breath. Every step toward the third curtain was like a mile. Speckles of golden light escaped from the rough edges of the cloth.

I told Hazel to stay behind me, as if she understood me. She moved in closer, panting. I was only a few steps away now. I placed my hand on the warm curtain, counted to three, and ripped it aside.

The acrid scent of gun smoke hit me first. In this room, a hospital bed was framed against an open window whose curtains were frozen as if the shadowcraft hit pause on a gust of wind. Someone lay in the bed. From the shape and air, it looked like a dead body. Solemnity and peace hung in the air around the bed.

Harris stood in the room with his gun drawn. The muzzle was in the middle of a flash, and a bullet hung frozen in the air. It aimed at Kay, still in her hospital gown. She ran at Harris with a knife raised.

Bo stood next to Harris, aiming his gun at someone else.

Natkaal hung from a silk thread on the ceiling, poised in the middle of a pendulum-like swing. The grasshopper's mouth was contorted into an angry curse.

I studied the room again. Why was everyone in here? Why were they gathered around a dead body?

I took a few cautious steps into the room. The dead man on the hospital bed loomed closer. Somehow, he held the answer to all of this. Somehow, when time resumed, his presence would contain the key.

The man looked familiar. His hair was a wave of silver. His feet nearly hung off the edge of the hospital bed. He was tall. And gangly…

I quickened my steps now and stood over the dead body. When I saw his face, my stomach dropped.

I've seen a lot of dead bodies in my line of work. Comes with the territory. Nobody, and I mean nobody, is ever prepared for death. It's not like you see in Hollywood, with dramatic music playing as you take your last breath and your loved ones weep over your body. The sad part is, that's what people expect, and when they truly experience death, it takes them completely off guard.

The face usually freezes in the middle of an emotion, like anger, shock, or disgust. Slowly, the body grows stiff as a board, piece by piece, muscle by muscle, and within hours, rigor mortis sets in. Aside from a jumpy limb or two and the absence of breathing, the body looks asleep. As the facial muscles relax, the face grows more neutral, more peaceful. The eyes are usually closed.

I've never seen a dead person with a smile on their face. The dead man's lips were pulled upward into a content, satisfied, and somewhat shit-eating grin. His face defied the laws of death and would probably haunt my dreams.

I checked the name on his wristband and cursed.

In front of me lay the body of Orman Misterka.

CHAPTER TWENTY-SEVEN

YOU WOULDN'T BELIEVE the curse words flying around my mind as I stared at Misterka. The damn cadaver was smiling as if to mock me.

Rage swelled in my chest, and I didn't know what to do with it. I suddenly wanted to punch something.

A voice was suddenly in the room with me.

"Don't be too upset, Lester."

A dazzle of gold flashed behind me. I turned to see a woman in dreadlocks. The hospital chaplain. Her dreads were tied in a neat ponytail that ran down her back. Instead of the business attire she had been wearing earlier, she was clad in golden armor—a smooth, glossy cuirass and gauntlets. A small but mighty rapier hung in a scabbard at her side. Behind her, moving translucently in the air was a pair of feathered wings. She smiled as she took a step toward me. "I'm sorry for all the subterfuge. Unfortunately, there was no other way."

I wanted to say something. I wanted to move, but my body locked into place. I opened my mouth, but only mumbling slipped out. I suppose that was the typical response upon seeing an angel for the first time. I especially didn't expect to meet one in a sterile, dark hospital room in the middle of madness.

"Yes, I am an angel," she said. "You've been on my radar for a long time, Lester."

I still had no clue what to say, but the shock and awe slowly wore off as Hazel trotted up to her. I had almost forgotten that my sweet pea was with me.

Laughing a hearty laugh, the angel bent down and gave the dog a loving rub behind the ears. Her armor clanked as she stood again. Her eyes focused outside, through the open window to the wall of lightning. Growling thunder rattled the plates on her mail. Her wings flapped quietly, sending down fuzzy golden orbs of light that danced around Misterka's cadaver and died on the white sheets near his feet.

"I've seen many achieve redemption," she said. "It never dawned on me that a necromancer might one day."

"Redemption?"

The woman shrugged as she turned to me. "I don't mean any offense," she said. "Just take it in the spirit in which it was intended. But necromancy is a dirty business, Lester."

"You got that right," I said, not wanting to litigate my past. I pointed to Hazel. "You brought me my dog."

"We heard your prayer. About Granny. In order for her to be okay, you've got to be okay. I have a feeling you're going to need Hazel."

She gave a loud, boisterous laugh. "Your prayer game needs some work, though. But I just want you to know that you were heard. You are always seen and always loved."

"Who are you?" I asked quietly.

"I am one of many guardian angels assigned to protect the city," she said. "I want you to know that we can't protect everyone. We just follow orders. I'm truly sorry about what happened to your wife and son. We wept over them; we wept for you."

I imagined her perched like a gargoyle on a city roof on a

rainy night, her wings tucked against her back as she wept in the rain, her tears mixing with the pouring raindrops. Maybe that's why angels cried—they couldn't save everyone.

The woman's voice was sincere and heartfelt. Every word she said seeped into my soul and made it bigger. I didn't know why, but I didn't think she was capable of telling a lie.

"I've never seen you," I said. "I don't know any supernaturals who have ever seen an angel."

"We are seen when we want to be seen. We reveal our presence only to those who we can do work to and through."

"I never got your name—"

"It's difficult to say," the woman said. "Quite a mouthful, really. Just call me Maia."

"Maia," I said, repeating the name. "Thank you."

Maia smiled again. "You figured out the pieces. About shadowcraft and lightcraft."

"It wasn't easy," I said, putting my hands on my hips and looking around the hospital room at the frozen carnage—at Natkaal hanging upside down, Harris firing his gun, and the cadaver on the bed. "Maia, how is all of this supposed to end?"

"That's up to you," the angel said quickly. She walked over to Natkaal, who was hanging on the silk thread. With a slash of her sword, she cut the thread. She brought a finger to her lip in a hush gesture and grinned. Then she turned to me, her face serious again.

"I don't have any further control," she said. "I've cast this lightcraft spell to give you a sharp warning."

"Warning?"

"You know that there are three uses for lightcraft, right?"

I nodded. Maia walked to the edge of the bed and studied the dead gangly man. "You'd do well to remember that lesson."

Now she was getting cryptic on me. I didn't exactly appreciate it.

"I know it's not what you want to hear, but I have done all I can do," she said.

I didn't know why, but I recalled the very first conversation I had with Maia, when I was sitting in the hospital chapel staring up at the stained-glass window. I pulled out the suncatcher of Hazel and studied the shiny glass.

"From the dark depths, light," I said, more for myself than for her. When I looked up at Maia again, she was gone.

"From the dark depths, light," I said again. "That's it. That's the answer to all of this."

Outside, the wall of lightning illuminated the room blue for a moment. Thunder shook the building in an ominous rumble.

And without further warning, time resumed.

CHAPTER TWENTY-EIGHT

The remaining half of a bang from Harris's pistol ripped through my ears. A feminine grunt mixed with it, followed by a hard slam. Kay lay on the floor, blood seeping from a hand. A curved knife lay several feet from her. Harris leveled his gun at her.

Then, Natkaal's voice started.

"—regret this, you stupid detective," Natkaal said. "What the—"

POW!

The grasshopper crashed to the floor and lay in a daze among two broken chairs. His human hands rubbed his head and he beat away the chairs with a quick buzz of his wings.

Kay screamed murder as she beheld her bloodied hand, every scream grating against my ears. Her brain was finally catching up with the fact that she had been shot. She applied pressure to the wound with a shaky palm, but the gesture was haphazard and ineffective. She yelped and cried in shock, saying, "No, no, no…"

On the hospital bed, Orman Misterka's eyes opened like a scene from a horror movie. In one fluid motion, the previously dead gangly man held up a palm toward the wall, spawned a jagged stitch back to the spirit world, and propelled himself into a powerful bicycle kick that sent Natkaal rag-dolling into the stitch. Time seemed to slow down as the grasshopper's ruby red eyes widened. The stitch closed before he knew what the hell had happened.

"Hi, Natkaal," the gangly man said, landing spryly on the floor. He stood up and straightened his hospital gown over his pale, naked body. "Goodbye, Natkaal."

"Whoa," Bo said, jumping back. "You're—you're—"

A familiar, sarcasm-laced, arrogant laugh started from the gangly man's mouth, quiet and breathy at first, but then loud and mocking. The man exposed all his teeth as he laughed. He shivered with laughter at first; his eyes closed, forcing out tears, and he beat his hand against the hospital bed. Then he threw his head back and let out hyena-like chortles.

Bo, Harris, and I looked at each other with pursed lips while we waited for Halgeron the Lich King to get the mockery out of his system. After what seemed like an eternity, the gangly man composed himself, wiped the tears from his eyes, and then gave me a slow clap with an approving nod. The white curtain from the open window flapped softly behind him.

"Another job well done, Lester," Halgeron said. He gave a quarter bow similar to the way Misterka had done. His voice was back to normal now—confident, haughty, with the not-so-subtle impression that he had better things to do.

"You're unbelievable," I said. "You really had me going. Whispering Pines Tuxedo Company, my foot. You fell and died on my front steps on purpose, didn't you? I thought I was gonna need a lawyer."

Halgeron cracked his neck. "If I were truly Mr. Misterka, a jury would have bled you dry, no doubt." The subject must have been too mundane for him because he quickly changed it. "This hospital is dreadful. A dead man can't get any rest in a place like this. All things considered, it is good to see you, gentlemen, though honestly, we've got to stop meeting like this. I'm so sick of that damn grasshopper, I don't know what to do. The only reason I haven't killed him is because it would kill you too, Lester."

I didn't know if I was supposed to be thankful or terrified.

"I'm not a coward," Halgeron continued. "That idiot really did a PR number on me. The whole spirit world probably thinks I have grasshopper-phobia or something. It'll take me a thousand years to undo this damage."

The Lich King turned his gaze at Kay now. His eyes were furious in the darkened room, narrowing like a predator locking onto its prey. "And I must decide what to do with you, Kay O'Malley."

His voice was cold now. Kay crawled away toward the safety of a little bathroom, but Harris kept his gun pointed at her. She bumped hard into a medical cart, and the cart toppled over, squealing as it vomited metal and plastic supplies across the floor.

"You unleashed demons into this world," Halgeron said. "The depths of your amateurishness know no bounds."

"I was…doing what I had to do," she said. She was sweating profusely and her hand spasmed involuntarily. "No one…will stop me."

In true amateur fashion, Kay's eyes went to the door for half a millisecond before turning back to Halgeron. Halgeron puffed upon seeing the covert gesture.

The Lich King held out a palm. Half a second later, Katsaroth burst into the room with his sword raised. The roach vanished into the jagged stitch of light that Halgeron created for him. The stitch closed before the roach could react.

Halgeron shook his head. He twirled a finger at Kay quickly. "Get on with it."

"With what?" Kay asked in a quick breath. She winced as she pressed her hand.

"Come on," Halgeron said, doing a few soft lunges, warming himself up. "I haven't seen the last of the grasshopper yet, have I? Go ahead and let's get the final act over with."

"Shit," she said under her breath. Her breathing was rapid and shallow now.

"I sensed the shadowcraft spell you initiated about a minute ago," Halgeron said. "You have no idea who you're dealing with, do you?"

Right on cue, the air grew electric again, raising the hairs on my neck and arms.

Halgeron motioned to Harris. The boyish detective lowered his gun.

Kay slipped a suncatcher out of her pocket with trembling fingers. With an unsteady lift, she jammed her last beacon of hope into the air and shouted in a pained wail, "Master! Come to me!"

A pillar of light appeared around Kay. Filaments of white energy bloomed from her wounded hand and closed around the blood like bandages. She wiggled her fingers, unable to believe the healing power of the spell. Her hand was slightly discolored but otherwise normal. She closed her fingers into a tight fist, her face settling into a hard, confident grin as the light pillar enveloped her and blinded us.

Something slammed into Bo, and the dead man let out a loud "oof!"

Before I could respond, something clocked me in the jaw. Something clocked Harris too. The detective and I were suddenly on top of each other, lying on the floor.

Hectic footsteps ran from the room. The light faded, leaving Harris and me tangled on the floor, and Bo and Halgeron staring at each other.

"That girl has spunk for days," Harris said, rubbing his jaw.

Harris and I disentangled from each other and I rose to

my feet, my head swimming. Something told me I didn't need to pursue Kay. Whatever she was up to, we'd find out shortly. As soon as I thought that, a high-pitched roar filled the air outside.

Bo and I ran to the window.

Outside, in the blue sky over the hospital's parking garage, a spear of golden light streaked across the city skyline like a whistling firework, screaming and gnashing sharp teeth. It was the same spear that had attacked us over the pancake house. It was slightly bigger than Natkaal's normal size.

I recognized it now as a deformed representation of Natkaal. The grasshopper demon screamed as it circled the sky in a mad loop.

"He just won't quit," Bo said, pulling his sunglasses down to get a good look at the grasshopper demon in his new form.

"If he won't quit, then we won't either," I said.

"Excellent plan, gentlemen," Halgeron said, slipping out of the hospital gown.

Bo scrunched his face up at the gangly man. "And what exactly are you doing, dog?"

Halgeron gave a quiet laugh. "Don't worry, this isn't a strip show. I'll keep our grasshopper friend busy."

The gangly man pointed to me. "I have unfinished business at your residence. Go home and collect my van. Get back here as quickly as you can."

I tilted my head at Halgeron. "Your van?" I asked.

"You'll understand once you unlock it," Halgeron said. The Lich King stood naked in the open window and gave a wolfish grin. "This is going to get fun." He fell backward out of the window.

Bo instinctively called the skeleton king's name, but the gangly man crossed his arms over his chest and fell out of sight. My heart skipped a beat.

Seconds later, the walls of the hospital shook and rattled as a deep voice roared. The roar sounded from far below but caught up to us as an enormous shadow darkened the room.

Halgeron had returned to his usual form. He was a giant lanky skeleton the size of the hospital. His skull alone was two stories tall. His teeth were encrusted with rubies and emeralds. Swirling runes danced across the surface of his alabaster skull like a high-definition animated movie. The skeleton king extended one of his hands. A silver gladius appeared, and he trounced across the parking lot, dodging around cars as he pointed the sword at Natkaal.

The grasshopper dove from the sky like a shrieking rocket. Halgeron raised his sword to strike, running at Natkaal. The two struck in a clash of brilliant yellow light.

"Good God," Harris said. "Those two are going to destroy the city."

"Natkaal is counting on that," I said. I grabbed the suncatcher in my interior pocket. Hazel's image stared at me from the glass.

At my feet, the real Hazel panted and whimpered.

I remembered Maia. She told me I'd need my dog…

I bent down. "How about a little excitement, sweet pea?" I asked.

"I don't like that tone in your voice," Bo said.

"Desperate times call for desperate measures," I said. "Kay summoned Natkaal from the depths of the spirit world. Lightcraft is a medium of light and energy."

"So?" Harris said.

"If Kay can channel energy, so can I."

I held the suncatcher up toward the ceiling and willed all of my energy into it. Hazel barked at me as both of our bodies became engulfed in a spiraling prism of golden light. Then the barking stopped. When my eyes adjusted, Hazel lay on the ground, sleeping.

"What'd you do to her?" Bo asked.

My heart skipped a beat as I waited, trusting the magic to do its job and assist me like Maia had insinuated.

Outside, a menacing, wall-shaking bark made my heart race.

We looked outside. A lens flare flashed in the sky for a moment, then faded away. A second spear of honeyed light streaked across the cloudy sky like a comet. It started high in the sky but descended rapidly. Natkaal and Halgeron, in the middle of an intense grapple, paused and stared. Halgeron disengaged and retreated from the grasshopper with cunning.

"I'll be a monkey's uncle," Bo said.

"Be careful what you say," Harris said, grinning. "It might just come true."

I stared at the sky, my heart hammering in my chest. The radiance encircling the spear intensified as the contours molded into place. First, I saw the triangular ears standing at attention. The cone-shaped snout that led the way. Fur bristling in the shimmering light. Finally, four strong legs that seemed to gallop through the sky in great big strides that covered several yards each.

Hazel's spirit was up there in the sky. My sweet pea barked and growled again as she charged at Natkaal.

CHAPTER TWENTY-NINE

For the first time during this adventure, I had caught Natkaal completely off guard. The grasshopper witnessed Hazel barreling toward him, sheathed in a frenzied beam of light, but he did not know how to respond. The demon gave an agonizing Wilhelm scream as Hazel clamped her jaws on one of his mosaicked wings. The wing sheared away from Natkaal's body with a sound like a paper lunch sack tearing.

The injury robbed the grasshopper of his balance mid-flight. Hazel and Natkaal tumbled through the sky, souls fighting souls, spiraling around each other in a phantasm of light. They landed soundlessly on the roof of the parking garage and a blinding flare ripped across the area.

Halgeron laughed and stomped toward the garage, raising his sword high over his head, enjoying the fight. The swirling runes on his alabaster skull increased their speed and intensity.

"You sent backup," he said, his voice rattling all my bones.

The giant skeleton king turned back toward the hospital in my direction. "The plan, Lester!" he cried. "Remember the plan! I'll protect your dog."

A biting gale from Halgeron's enormous mouth blew me back a few inches and flapped my winter coat about.

"If you don't protect her, I'm coming after you next!" I shouted.

Halgeron nodded before leaping onto the top floor of the parking garage and landing with a boom. It was a miracle the structure didn't crumble; the skeleton must have been lighter than he looked. It definitely explained his speed.

Natkaal used his powerful hind legs to make a great leap into the sky just before Halgeron brought his sword down on the insect demon's thorax. Halgeron and Hazel stood next to each other, two comrades ready for war. Hazel bent low to the ground, her hackles raised and teeth bared. Halgeron readied his sword, taunting Natkaal with a string of curse words I won't repeat.

I wrapped the suncatcher tightly in my fingers. I projected an image of Kay onto the canvas of my mind's eye. The light-craft energy was all around me. I directed it with my thoughts.

A vision of Kay came to me. A lucid image with tattered borders whirled across my mind, showing me what I wanted to see: the woman was running through the hospital cafeteria, weaving around tables in the dark. I felt her fear, but also her elation and smugness with herself for avoiding death. I sensed all of her emotions as one tangled, insecure ball. I felt sorry for her again.

"Kay is in the cafeteria," I said quickly to Harris. "You've got to disable her. If you do, we can make Natkaal disappear. Trust me."

"I'll get it done," the boyish detective said.

Harris gave a sweaty fist bump to Bo and me. I could tell the boyish detective was scared out of his wits to go stalking after Kay in the dark by himself. I would have been too. Who knew what untold, unspeakable wonders were waiting in the bowels of this hospital now? Part of me felt guilty for sending him on what could have been a suicide mission, but I would have done the same for him without hesitation, just like he was doing for me now. That was the mark of true friendship. We had a plan, and all we had to do was execute it if we wanted to get out of this alive.

"Watch your back," I said to him.

"Always, Lester."

We stared at each other for a moment, not knowing if we'd ever see each other again. Then, the detective charged into the darkness, leading the way with his gun pointed ahead.

In the sky, Hazel and Natkaal took turns darting at each other and missing. One of the grasshopper's wings dangled limply on his side, but his springbox legs launched him into the air just in time to avoid Halgeron's sword.

"Come on, sweet pea," I said. "Don't let him hurt you."

As if she heard me, Hazel dodged a downward swipe by a sharp insect leg. She pivoted and slammed into Natkaal. The grasshopper bellowed in pain.

"Atta girl!" I cried, pumping a fist.

"We've got to get home," Bo said, watching the fight with concern. "It's going to take too long if we drive."

I told Bo to pick up Hazel's sleeping physical body.

"We've got to keep her safe," I said.

Since Hazel's spirit was in the sky, we had to protect her physical body. If something happened to it, she would die. But the soul was everlasting and eternal. I knew in my heart of hearts that nothing could hurt her up there in the sky—not even Natkaal.

"She's safe with me," Bo said, taking Hazel's brindled body into his arms.

I slid out my razor blade. "We'll take a shortcut."

I traced a quick cut along my palm. The portal to the spirit world opened up and we jumped through without hesitation. The hazy, sulfuric landscape sprang up around us.

I imagined my home, and another stitch of light appeared a few feet ahead. We were just about to jump through when a hand stopped me.

It was CeCe. Her rose-gold sword hung on her scabbard,

and the foul, fetid wind of the spirit world whispered against the base of her red couture dress. She smiled at me.

"Good job finding Halgeron," she said.

"Can't talk now," I said.

"We'll talk and walk," she said.

Together, Bo, CeCe, and I jumped into the stitch, into the hallway in my foyer. A welcome whoosh of fresh, furnaced air hit us as the stitch closed. The transoms over my front door let down slants of somber winter afternoon light. It felt good to be in the comfort of my home, if only for a moment.

I ran to my radiator and swiped the key fob that had belonged to Orman Misterka. I flung my front door open and ran down to the street where the white cargo van was parked on the curb in front of my house. Bo and CeCe trailed behind me.

I pointed the key fob at the door, driving my thumbnail into the unlock button. The van horn chirped as the locks disengaged and the fog lights flashed orange in acceptance of the fob's signal.

All around us, my street was also frozen. A few neighbors were paused while walking to their cars.

I only heard one set of footsteps when I should have heard two. Bo joined me as I reached the van.

CeCe stood slack-jawed in my front yard. Her dress was a streak of scarlet in the snow.

"Let's go," I cried, motioning CeCe to the van.

"I can't believe him," she said. What little color was left in her dead face was completely gone now. She was practically translucent.

"What is it?" Bo asked.

"Halgeron is a dirty, vile—"

"CeCe," I said.

"I'll kill him," CeCe said, incredulously. "I swear on every wave in my lake that I—will—kill—him."

She threw her hands up in defeat, glancing ironically

around the block as if someone else was watching her and she wanted their approval. "I mean, can you believe this? This is just unbelievable. Unbelievable!"

I crossed my arms and stared at her.

It took her a moment to realize that I had no idea what she was talking about.

"That's not a van," she said.

I studied the white cargo van, looking it up and down. "Looks like one to me."

"Well, I mean, it is, but it's more than just that. Seriously, I'll kill him if he doesn't teach me how he did this."

With a quick stride, CeCe blazed past me, grabbed the sliding door, and pulled it open. A loud metallic whine echoed down the street.

I don't know what I had expected to see. Maybe a rack full of tuxedos, garment bags, or shelving units. Something befitting of The Whispering Pines Tuxedo Company, even though the company itself was a ruse. And sure, there *was* a rack of plastic-wrapped tuxedos, poplin shirts and bowties hanging in the van's cargo space. But that was not all there was.

A wave of sickly green light washed over CeCe's face as she put a single hand on her hip and looked back at me with a knowing grin.

A sage green swirling light flowed out of the van in rhythmic pulses. As my eyes adjusted to the brightness, I spotted a huge orb of light floating in the cargo space among the tuxedo garments. The orb was as big as my head. As we neared, the rhythm grew faster and more erratic. The light had a music of its own, a frenzied, dissonant grating that reminded me of an avant-garde jazz ensemble where all the players in the horn section played the wrong notes, and the drummer played the wrong key signature, and the piano player just banged the keys for the hell of it.

"Now I know why you want to kill him," I said flatly.

"Pretty amazing, isn't it?" she asked. "In an ironic way, of course."

Shifting Hazel in his big arms, Bo tilted his head down and stared at the green orb over the top of his sunglasses before giving out a long whistle.

"So this is what they look like," the dead man said. "He hid this thang in plain sight too."

I've seen a lot in my almost fifty years on this planet. Some of it has surprised me; some of it has scared me out of my mind; some of it has made me cry; some of it has made my heart bigger. But there was still an infinitely long list of things in this dark and complicated world that I hadn't seen yet.

I could now cross a phylactery off that list.

CHAPTER THIRTY

"I'M DRIVING," CeCe said, climbing into the driver seat.

"I'm riding in the back for once," Bo said. He set Hazel's body in the workspace of the van, climbed in, and rolled the door shut. I climbed into the passenger seat and tossed CeCe the key fob. She cranked the key in the ignition and the van's engine purred on. I didn't even have a chance to put my seatbelt on before CeCe slammed on the accelerator and rocketed the van down the street.

"Damn, girl!" Bo cried. He clutched a tuxedo hanging on a rack and held on for dear life.

"I haven't driven since I died," she said, a slow but mischievous grin spreading across her face. "And it feels amazing!"

I clicked my seatbelt and murmured a small prayer.

"*You* might be dead, but I hope I still have some time among the living left," I said.

"Don't trust my driving skills?" CeCe asked. "Don't worry. We're taking a shortcut."

She clenched the steering wheel and hunched over slightly, narrowing her eyes. A dozen yards away, a crevasse traced itself into the sky in the middle of the street. The dark, hazy plane of the spirit world loomed ahead.

"Hang on to something," CeCe said, pushing harder on the accelerator. The engine whined. I held on to the armrest on the passenger door as tightly as I could.

The van broke into the spirit world, jostling over rocks and uneven land. The dark orange sky with bubbling phantoms passed over the windshield like a pall.

Something smacked against the side of the van. From the sound of it, it left a giant dent.

Flying alongside the van were insect demons.

A giant ladybug with a ghoulish face, deformed fangs, and slingshot flew next to the van. In its slingshot was a rock the size of my head.

The insect demon fanned away from the van, squinted one of its sickly eyes, and flung the rock at the window. I ducked as the rock struck the glass at a low angle, shattering it before bouncing away.

"These demons always have to make my life so miserable," CeCe said angrily.

I glanced over at the ladybug demon whose red and black wings were buzzing furiously as it swiped a giant rock off the ground and into its giant leather-strapped slingshot.

"CeCe," I said, dragging out her name. This time, there wouldn't be a window to protect me.

A lich in a long, tattered cloak and a black sword appeared in the air above the ladybug. The ladybug looked up just in time to see the sword pierce its face. The lich surfed the dying insect demon's body down to the ground. He waved at CeCe and me.

"So little faith, Lester," CeCe said, tapping me playfully on the shoulder. "Oooh, look at the dashboard!"

In the place of the radio was a white box with two big buttons. One was red and one was black. The red button had a handwritten sticky note below it that read “Attack.” The black button had a note that read “Absorb.”

“You’ve got to be kidding me,” I said, pondering the buttons. Another rock struck the side of the van, pulling my attention back to the fight.

CeCe gripped the steering wheel tightly again and hunched over, focusing on the land ahead.

I glanced in the rearview mirror. A horde of insects barreled toward us like something out of a zombie movie. They ran, gnashing their teeth and throwing up a furious cloud of dust into the burnt-orange sky that blocked out the shrieking, popping phantoms.

"Faster!" I cried.

"I'm at top speed!”

I glanced back again. We weren't going to make it. Even if we did, we would bring a horde of insect demons into St. Louis with us. That was how this mess started in the first place.

"Bo!" I cried. "Can you open the back door?”

The shining, brilliant light of the phylactery washed out all except the dead man’s bald head.

"Yup,” he said.

I glanced at the dashboard again, at the buttons.

"Somehow I think the skeleton king had this all planned out," I said. “Bo, open both of the back doors.”

A second later, Bo unlatched both doors and they swung open, giving another glimpse of the rushing demon horde between the flapping rear doors.

Without hesitation, I pushed the button for "Attack."

The button depressed into its groove like it was oiled with butter. The orb hummed violently and Bo cursed, ducking with his hands over his bald head.

The orb rattled off a salvo of several dozen missiles of pale green light. The missiles snaked between the flapping rear doors, leaving streaks of green behind them. Each missile homed in on an insect demon and struck it, releasing another salvo of smaller needles of light that zipped high into the sky, and then down onto the horde, where they exploded like cluster bombs. The demons screamed and the initial impact stopped the wall of them dead in their tracks.

"What the hell was that, and where can I order one?" Bo asked. "Daaaaayum!"

The orb quaked and let off another salvo. The impact struck the demons like fireworks. The insects fell back and wailed in agony as the van ramped off a rock and jumped back into the world of the living, into the hospital parking lot.

"Tell Halgeron I want one of those for Christmas," I said, grinning as the stitch closed behind us.

"Deal," CeCe said, jerking the wheel to the left.

A spectacle of cars, trucks, and vans dazzled by as she wove through the parking lot and toward the garage. On the top floor of the garage, Natkaal kicked Hazel in the back, sending my dog flying off the edge.

I leaned out the window and shouted Hazel's name. She must have heard me. The dog barked and careened across the parking lot like a burning spear, making a crescent through the sky as she rocketed toward Natkaal.

Natkaal and Halgeron circled each other. Halgeron gave a strong swing, but the grasshopper ducked under the sword and used his springbox legs to launch himself into the skeleton king's sternum. The impact knocked the sword out of Halgeron's hands. In a smooth motion, Natkaal grabbed the sword and swung it at Halgeron's head.

Hazel smashed into Halgeron just in time. The skeleton toppled off the parking garage like a bag of bones, spilling into a clearing of snow. Hazel narrowly missed the swipe from the sword and raced away.

Natkaal gripped the sword tight and leaped high, pointing the sword at Halgeron. The grasshopper dove with the sword pointed at Halgeron, who was struggling in the snow below.

CeCe swerved and braked, facing the side of the van toward Halgeron. The deafening sound of skidding tires filled my ears.

"Bo, open the door!" she cried.

Bo ripped the side door open and ducked.

"Lester! Now!" CeCe yelled.

I jammed my finger against the "Absorb" button.

Instantly, a sage hyperbeam erupted from the orb, rocking the van and shaking every panel violently. The column made rapid right angles as it sped toward Natkaal, and Natkaal sped toward Halgeron.

The beam slammed into Natkaal just before the grasshopper struck Halgeron. The gladius went flying and stuck in the snow near the skeleton king.

The impact was like a wall that absorbed all of Natkaal's energy. The grasshopper demon's eyes bulged out of his head. He gave a terrified cry as invisible hands yanked his body, pulling it like a string of spaghetti toward the van.

"This can't be," he said. "How did you hide your phylactery? The lightcraft was supposed to work. Damn, damn, damn!"

The grasshopper cried out again as his light-ridden body stretched and stretched and stretched. He began to turn into a long comet with no form. The last traces of his grasshopper body disappeared into the light. Now he was pure energy.

His voice lingered. "I will never forgive you for this, necromancer! Lich King! Lich girl! Dead man! Idiot detective! I will become an archdemon one way or the other. My plan succeeded regardless, for the archdemons will remember what I have done in a thousand years. I won't be denied. I won't—"

An obnoxious slurping sound escaped from the van, like someone sucking the last droplets of a soft drink through a straw. The phylactery's hungry orb sucked in the long spaghetti strand of light until every ounce of Natkaal's spirit disappeared into its vibrant green depths.

"You think you can contain me? I spit in your face, Halgeron!"

The grasshopper gave a defiant horse whinny laugh before something violently cut it short.

The orb let out an earthshaking, van-rattling belch, long and disgustingly deep.

Then all was quiet.

CHAPTER THIRTY-ONE

TIME RESUMED.

Frightened screams reverberated throughout the hospital parking lot, followed by whirring sirens.

Halgeron had morphed into the human body of Orman Misterka. None of these people running across the parking lot had had any clue that he had been a giant skeleton just a few seconds ago. Aside from a few banged-up cars, you wouldn't have even known a fight had taken place.

The gangly man gave Bo, CeCe, and me a quarter bow.

CeCe slammed the driver side down and stomped toward Halgeron.

"I thought you'd be happier to see me," he said, holding up two open palms. CeCe stopped a few feet short of him and put her hands on her hips. "You have no idea what you put me through. Can we not do that again?"

"That was a once-in-a-thousand-year spell, Cecelia," Halgeron said, grinning. "I'll show you every step. You may need it someday."

Bo and I climbed out of the van. Hazel, whose physical body had been sleeping in the cargo space, stirred awake, stretched, and gave a big yawn. I bent down and nuzzled her.

"That was incredible, sweet pea," I said, a tear in my eye. I gave my dog a big hug, and I held her tight for a few seconds. She licked me, covering my face with warm saliva, and I laughed.

"Hazel, the demon warrior," Bo said. "I think you deserve a few rawhide bones and a week's worth of belly rubs for that performance, girl."

Bo, Hazel, and I jogged over to meet CeCe and Halgeron. Together, we surveyed the innocent bystanders who had gathered in crowds around the parking lot, talking to each other about what the hell had just happened—no, they hadn't imagined it—no, this couldn't have been a joke—and—my God, what were those things moving in the shadows of the hallways?

"I owe you a favor, Lester," Halgeron said. "If it makes you feel proud, you are the only person on this entire planet and in the history of existence that I knew I could trust with my phylactery."

The comment took my breath away. "I'll take that as a compliment."

"Natkaal was so hell-bent on finding my phylactery that he made two critical mistakes. First, he correctly assumed that you would be embroiled in the middle of this."

"I have you to thank for that," I said sarcastically.

"He also rightly bypassed the wards in your home," Halgeron said. "A very clever trick."

"Those wards were wizard-grade," I said.

"And they were quite effective. When Natkaal supervised the installation of the wards in your home, he correctly surmised that neither he nor any of his minions could enter your home with the intent to harm you. But the weakness in the ward was the intent. Natkaal and his minions *could* enter your home, but only if their intent was not to harm you."

"Their intent was to find you," I said.

Halgeron pointed a finger at me and clucked his tongue.

"Exactly. They couldn't enter your home to do you harm, but they could enter to listen and monitor. Again, quite an ingenious loophole. That grasshopper always was a clever one. If I were you, I'd give Hank Garbo a call and have him upgrade the wards so that *nothing* can enter your home without your express permission. Those types of wards are inconvenient, but in your line of work, Lester, you need the ultimate protection."

The Lich King extended a hand. "So long, and thanks for another thrill."

I took his warm, cadaverous hand. "May the next thrill never come."

I glanced back at the van. It was gone. I hoped I would never see it again, though I wouldn't have minded a missile-shooting, demon-eating orb for myself. When you practiced the dark art, a weapon like that could come in real handy.

"What did you do to Natkaal?" I asked.

"I had to absorb the grasshopper demon into my phylactery," Halgeron said. "He's enjoying his new prison right now. It comes at a significant cost to me, but it's nothing I can't handle. Go ahead and live your life, Lester. I can guarantee that my soul will contain him at least until your human life is over. Beyond that, fate will tell. The archdemons will have me marked, no doubt. They may take action to rescue him, but there's been so much drama with you lately that they won't risk it for fear of irritating the angels. His antics are sure to have gotten the attention of the archdemons, though. Since Natkaal helped you kill the archdemon Elziel, they're not fond of the grasshopper, but demons speak the language of strength. Natkaal showed tremendous strength in the spirit world, and he united demons in a way I've never seen before. That won't be lost on the archdemons. We rejoice today, but in a thousand years at the next molting season, it may be Natkaal who has the last laugh. He may have already won today."

The words sent a shiver down my spine.

"But if I die, he dies," I said.

"Unless the archdemons wish to transfuse his blood with their own," Halgeron said. "It's next-level magic. There is always a way to do anything you want, though there is a terrible cost. But as I said, you are free now."

I sighed with relief. Part of me was grateful that I didn't have to play cat and mouse with the grasshopper again. Part of me was sad for the fact that it had to happen in the first place. Natkaal had been a friend, and even though he turned evil, I still couldn't let go of the adventures I spent with the mischief maker, the lessons he taught me—about the dark art and about the cold, hard realities of life as a necromancer.

Memories of Natkaal would forever be a tangle of difficult emotions to unravel. Maybe I'd never truly make peace with how this went down. But it was in the past now, and I was ready to move on.

"The grasshopper's really gone?" Bo asked.

"Super gone," CeCe said. She punched me playfully on the shoulder. "Thanks for the help."

"Maybe take some driving lessons before you get behind the wheel again," I joked.

A squadron of police cars careened into the parking lot. We watched silently as they skidded to a stop and officers charged out, running toward the hospital entrance.

Halgeron pointed toward the building, making a long face. "Lester, you'd better attend to your friend."

When I looked over at CeCe and Halgeron, they were gone.

"Harris," Bo and I said at the same time.

We found Harris in the cafeteria, holstering his gun as two officers slid a white sheet over a female body under a table. He walked away, shaking his head.

Upon seeing us, his face brightened a little, but not much. I was relieved to see him alive. Just over his shoulder, I stole a glance at a limp hand holding a suncatcher of a grasshopper. My eyes widened.

"Is that—"

Harris nodded.

I put a hand on his shoulder and gripped it tightly.

Harris shook his head. "Fate smiled upon me," he said quietly. "I found her in the cafeteria, just like you said. We got into a terrible fight. She fought me like a wild animal. I've never seen anyone so enraged. I didn't want to kill her. It was impossible to see in the dark. Impossible to get a good shot, you understand. Then, suddenly, she dropped like a sack of potatoes. She just—dropped dead. I've never seen anything like it. Saved me a bullet, though I didn't want to see her die."

"It must have been the breaking of the lightcraft spell," I said. "When Halgeron absorbed Natkaal, it probably broke Kay's mind."

"Another amateur necromancer in the spirit world," Bo said. He took off his sunglasses sadly as he surveyed the white sheet that held Kay's body. "We just never can save 'em, can we, boss man?"

A few seconds of silence passed.

"What happened, Lester?" Harris asked.

I told him about the fight.

The boyish detective shook his head again. "Good God. At least it's over now."

The three of us stood solemnly in a moment of silence for Kay as first responders lifted her lifeless body onto a gurney and wheeled it ceremoniously to some dreadful morgue deep, deep inside the belly of this great hospital beast.

We found Granny still asleep in her hospital bed. She had slept through the apocalypse. Peter, one of her sons, sat by her bedside, holding her hand.

He rose when he saw me. I embraced him. He asked what happened. I told him I didn't know, but that I was glad that Granny would be okay. I told Peter she was a tough old bird, to take good care of her, and that Bo and I would look out for her when she came home. He appreciated that. As I left the room, I wished I could have told him the truth. But like Granny liked to say—there are just some things that you can't do anything about.

As Bo, Hazel and I drove away from the hospital, I didn't even look at the place in the rearview mirror. If I never saw another hospital again, it would be too soon.

CHAPTER THIRTY-TWO

"Wow, Daddy, you have the craziest luck of anyone I know," Marlese said on the other end of the phone.

I had her on speakerphone. I was setting the dining room table.

In the kitchen, Bo whistled as he clanged a few pots around. The spicy aroma of a new batch of Tabasco chicken noodle soup wafted out of the kitchen. The soup bubbled in a stock pot and the fan over the stove hummed at full speed. The house smelled divine—of celery and spice.

I had just finished telling Marlese everything. It had been a week since it all happened.

Granny was home from the hospital and back to her normal self. She was still moving a little slowly, but her mind was back. I knew that her body would soon follow. I had invited her over for dinner.

I had also invited Harris. He told me he had someone for me to meet. I assumed he was bringing a girlfriend, so I set an extra place at the table.

"Anyway, I'm sorry about the tuxedos," I said to Marlese. "Bo and I will make it up to you. We'll find something by the end of the month, I promise."

Marlese hesitated. "I don't think that will be necessary."

I was in the middle of setting out a bowl. I paused, arching an eyebrow. "What do you mean?"

The doorbell rang. My front porch spider beamed a black-and-white image of a delivery man. He carried two thick bags that looked like cocoons. I grabbed my phone and walked cautiously to the door.

"Lester Broussard?" the man asked. He handed me the black leather bags and told me to sign my name.

"Right on time, like he promised," Marlese said as I dragged the bags into my living room.

"Like *who* promised?"

"Your friend, the skull man," Marlese said sarcastically. "He called to personally apologize to me. We were supposed to be planning *my* special day, remember?"

I didn't believe her at first. Halgeron calling Marlese? Sheeeeet...now I had seen everything. The skeleton king certainly had class...when he wanted to.

I unzipped the garment bags. The first tuxedo was handsomely cut. The black jacket, crafted from high-quality wool, was a classic cut with clean lines and a sleek notched lapel with a satin sheen. The vest was of deep violet herringbone with a matching tie. The vest and tie had a sophisticated patterned texture that I had to examine closely to see clearly. A repeating diagonal of skulls were expertly woven into the lustrous fabric. The skulls were tastefully designed and only caught the light if you were paying attention. And, of course, there was a crisp white shirt made from Egyptian cotton, complemented with glossy violet buttons and golden cufflinks that added a touch of opulence.

The second tuxedo was considerably larger to accommodate Bo's large frame, but it followed the same style. Attached to the breast pocket was an expensive-looking card printed on thick, creamy paper. I slipped it out of the envelope and read the neat handwriting. The word “Sheeeeet” took up half the card. After it was the following message:

Lester Broussard and Bo Holloway in tuxedos? A special occasion, indeed!

I'm a man of my word. Enjoy your daughter's special day.

P.S. Give my love to Hazel as well. She was a most splendid battle companion.

In the bottom of the second garment bag was a plastic bag wrapped with a red ribbon. In it were two femur-sized rawhide bones.

I called Hazel. She trotted into the foyer, and her tail went crazy upon seeing the bones. I gave her one.

Bo entered the foyer and put a fist into his mouth. "Now *that's* a clean-cut suit!” He held up the tuxedo to his chest and said, “California, look out!"

"Well?" Marlese asked after a while. I forgot she was still on the phone.

"You're going to be very happy with how Bo and I look," I said.

"But what about Mom and Nana?" Marlese asked, concerned.

I smiled. Now that the lich lakes were back open, I'd be able to tell my wife and mother about the tuxes and relay Marlese’s questions to them again.

"I have a feeling your mother and grandmother will also be happy. Bo and I will try the tuxes on later tonight and send you some pics.”

From the other end of the phone, my grandson Malcolm called out to me. I talked to my little man for a moment and told him I loved him before Marlese came back on the line. I told her I would call her in a few days.

The doorbell rang again. Granny stood at the front step with another plate of peach cobbler.

"Tell me something good,” she said. I kissed her on the

cheek and took the plate, helping her over the threshold. I asked her how she was feeling as we walked into the kitchen.

"Better and stronger every day, baby. I'll be extra glad when I get back to the senior center."

Granny and I had talked since her abduction. She asked me what happened. I decided to come clean. I started from the beginning, about my journey into necromancy. The very act of listening to my story exhausted her. Then she told me that it sure explained all the strange things going on at my house. I asked if she could keep a secret; she grinned and told me just this once, she'd have to. It would trash her reputation at the senior center if she started talking about demons and necromancers all of a sudden. They'd think she was going senile and would withhold all the juicy gossip out of pity, and no lawd, that wouldn't do. She told me she'd be doing a lot of praying for me and Bo, and that was being kind.

From that moment on, Granny and I understood each other. As for Bo…

Granny stopped in the kitchen doorway. Next to a giant pot of soup, Bo was chopping celery and dancing in place. He sensed her gaze. He turned around and startled, embarrassed.

"Hey, Mrs. Powell." Bo took off his apron and lowered his eyes.

"You got something to tell me?" Granny asked in a tough voice.

Bo looked up at her, terrified.

Granny's face softened as she wagged her finger at him. "You're not Lester's cousin from Tennessee. And you can't exactly eat on account of some…unusual circumstances, can you?"

Bo glanced at me nervously.

Granny broke the silence.

"It all makes sense now," she said, holding out her hands for a hug. "And wouldn't nobody believe me if I told them anyway. So get over here, big man. I will love you just like I love Lester."

Bo practically ran across the kitchen and pulled the old woman into a hug. They shared it for a few moments. I stood holding the plate of peach cobbler, grinning from ear to ear.

"Thanks, Mrs. Powell," Bo said.

"Call me Granny," she said. She craned her head around his arms to look at the cutting board. "Boy, those celery bits are raggedy. Give me that knife."

Bo and Granny puttered in the kitchen as I put the plate of peach cobbler in the refrigerator. Hazel was on my heels the entire way to the refrigerator with the giant rawhide bone in her mouth. She whined at me, looking up expectantly. She was waiting for her slice of cobbler too. She'd get it before long.

The doorbell rang again. My spider beamed a vision to me. Harris stood on the doorstep. My spider didn't care about him because he was on my VIP list. However, next to him stood a muscular, blonde-haired woman with a cropped haircut.

"Who the hell is that?" I said, not realizing I had spoken out loud. I disengaged the deadbolt and opened the door. The boyish detective grinned mischievously at me. My eyes went to the woman. She looked painfully uncomfortable, like my house was the last place in the world she wanted to be. She didn't meet my eyes.

"Hey, Lester," Harris said, extending a hand.

"Hey," I said. "I see you brought company."

Harris shrugged. "Yes, I believe you've met."

The woman said hello in a deep voice. Still, she would not meet my eyes.

"I'm sorry?" I asked. "I don't think I know you."

Harris let himself in and took me by the shoulder as we walked down the hallway. The woman followed behind us slowly, glancing around my foyer.

"You see, there's this necromancer technique that's super effective, but rarely used. I think you've heard of it, Lester."

"I have?" I asked slowly.

Harris spoke as if it were the most mundane thing in the world. "You know, you go to a mortician, ask for a dead body you can borrow for a while. Then you make a deal with a grim reaper and a lich, and next thing you know—boom. You got yourself in undead servant."

I stopped cold.

"It wasn't quite like that," Harris said. "But pretty close. Our big skeleton friend wasn't happy about a certain entrant into the spirit world upon her death. He was so infuriated with said entrant that he called a meeting with a certain—I don't know, hospital chaplain—and yours truly to talk about what should be done about said entrant. She caused a real big problem. And she's a total amateur."

"You got that right," I said, giving a long stare at Kay O'Malley in her new undead body. It was the perfect body for a future cop—muscular yet still intensely feminine. I got the feeling that Kay could do some serious damage with her new form.

"Halgeron and the laughing angel came to an agreement," Harris continued. "They said that our friend here had to do community service for all the lightcraft she cast and the damage she caused. Apparently, angels are big on community service. Said community service involved coming back to life as the second member of the St. Louis Police Department Paranormal Crimes Division. She's required to pass the police academy, upon which she will join me as my partner. She will have to help me solve at least 250 murders before Halgeron and the laughing angel decide what's next for her."

He turned and spoke to her playfully. "Turns out shadowcraft and lightcraft are dirty businesses."

"Don't rub it in," Kay said.

"How do you know she's not going to cross you?" I asked, not taking my eyes off Kay.

"She's on strict probation," Harris said. "If she even so much as thinks about double-crossing me or anyone on the side of good, Halgeron and the angels have a very unpleasant future set aside for her. On a more positive note, they praised her spunk and energy. They want her to do something good with her skill set."

Harris turned to Kay and tilted his head at me. "Kay, I think there was one thing that you needed to do, remember?"

Kay finally met my eyes. I was used to seeing her tangles of auburn hair and bright green eyes. Instead, intense Pacific-blue eyes stared at me.

"I'm sorry, Lester. It was never my intent to mess things up so badly. I just wanted to see my husband again."

"We all want to see our loved ones again," I said. I paused for a beat. "Did you succeed?"

Her face brightened with a quick smile that told me all I needed to know. Good grief, the things we necromancers do to see our families again.

"I accept your apology," I said. "Now that you're on our side, call me and Bo any time you need. If you're helping Harris, then it would be my pleasure to help you."

She nodded. Then she sniffed. "It smells amazing in here."

"That would be Bo's famous Tabasco chicken noodle soup," Harris said, sidling into the kitchen. "He's got a few things to teach you as part of your undead servant training. He's going to give you the recipe."

"Cooking wasn't in the agreement," Kay said. "You're going to cook your own damn food."

Harris shrugged and flashed me a winsome smile. "It was worth a shot."

We entered the kitchen and Granny cheered upon seeing Harris, saying how nice it was to see the handsome detective again.

Among all of the hubbub, Bo caught my eye and nodded to me. I nodded back.

"I'd say we put the can on this shizzle," the dead man said.

"Good way of putting it," I said.

We made our way, laughing, into the dining room, where Granny and Bo served Bo's world-famous soup.

As we ate, a golden light twinkled in the dining room window. No one saw it except me.

I excused myself and walked through the rubble on my back porch. Bo, my neighbor Ant'ny, and me were rebuilding the porch from where I had blown Katsaroth through the wall. The mess was unsightly, and it would be a few weeks until we were done. I passed through a giant roach demon-sized hole from my kitchen onto the porch. I stepped around power tools, freshly bundled lumber, and plastic wrap, and I slipped outside.

The snow had almost melted, replaced with brown grass that looked like a bad hair day. Only a few timid white patches remained here and there on the sidewalk, watery at the edges. The sunbeams were warm against my skin and the air was crisp. Soon, winter would give up the ghost; it was just a matter of days before the arrival of green grass and gay, colorful flowers.

Maia was leaning against the tree in my backyard. She still wore her plate mail, and it glowed with golden light. Her dreads hung freely, resting on the shoulders of her mail. Seeing me, she pushed off the tree and met me halfway down the paved brick walkway that cut through my yard.

"Thank you for everything," I said.

Maia smiled. "You survived," she said. "I'm really glad to see it, Lester. You're a quick thinker."

"Quick thinking is an automatic reflex after you've been threatened with death as many times as I have," I said. "Listen. We've got an extra space at the table. We'd love to have you."

Gratitude radiated in the angel's eyes. The invitation touched her. But she shook her head.

"I'd love to, but angels don't need to eat," she said. "I merely came to wish you well. And to ask a favor. I hate to trouble you, but…"

I listened. She kept it brief—something about meeting her on another side of town in a few weeks. She handed me an address and a date and time on a slip of paper. I tucked it in my shirt pocket. I told her she could count on me.

"You sure you don't want to join?" I said, tilting my head toward the house. "There's an old woman in there who would love to meet an angel. It would make your day. Trust me."

A slow smile spread across Maia's face, and then she laughed that hearty, full-throated laugh that made me laugh with her. I closed my eyes in delight, and when I opened them, she was gone. Only little speckles of golden light remained, caught by the wind, carried up into the branches of my maple tree before winking out.

Sometimes with supernatural folks, you never could tell. I had a feeling I'd be seeing a lot more of Maia soon. That didn't bother me at all.

I watched the last of the golden speckles disappear one by one in the azure sky as a lukewarm winter breeze blew across the yard. Then, I dug my hands into my pockets and smiled all the way back to the house.

MORE URBAN FANTASY BY MICHAEL LA RONN

Love Lester's stories and want to be notified when the next one launches? Join Michael's Fantasy Fan Club.

Want to check out more urban fantasy titles by Michael? Visit www.michaellaronn.com/books.

MEET MICHAEL LA RONN

Michael La Ronn has written many books of science fiction & fantasy. Michael was born and raised in St. Louis, Missouri where *The Good Necromancer* series takes place.

In 2012, a life-threatening illness made him realize that storytelling was his #1 passion. He's devoted his life to writing ever since, making up whatever story makes him fall out of his chair laughing the hardest. Every day.

To get updates when he releases new work + other bonuses, sign up by visiting www.michaellaronn.com/fanclub.

www.ingramcontent.com/pod-product-compliance
Lightning Source LLC
Chambersburg PA
CBHW021624030826
48979CB00038B/2354/J

* 9 7 9 8 8 8 5 5 1 1 5 4 4 *